THOSE
WHO KNEW

THOSE WHO KNEW

Idra Novey

VIKING

VIKING
An imprint of Penguin Random House LLC
375 Hudson Street
New York, New York 10014
penguinrandomhouse.com

ISBN: 9780525560432 (hardcover)
ISBN: 9780525560449 (ebook)

Printed in the United States of America
1   3   5   7   9   10   8   6   4   2

Set in Adobe Garamond Pro

For Boaz and Lázaro

I

*In the aging port city
of an island nation
near the start of the new millennium*

Precisely a week after the death of Maria P. was declared an accident, a woman reached into her tote bag and found a sweater inside that didn't belong to her. Standing at the register in the supermarket, she had reached in for her wallet, which was there, as were her keys and the bundled up green bulk of her scarf.

Only now there was also this worn black sweater. I don't remember walking away from my cart, she told the cashier, but I must have, and somebody stuck this in my bag by mistake.

She held the sweater up over the register and saw that a white zigzag ran across the front like the pulse line on a heart monitor. The broadness of the neckline brought to mind a sweater she'd worn in college. She'd worn it constantly until she lost it at the last protest before the election that finally brought Cato down. She'd liked the open feeling of the sweater's neckline, though it was always shifting and, like her confidence then, had required continual adjustment.

You could just keep it, the cashier said.

No, no—it isn't mine. She handed off the sweater, and while the cashier balled it up once more, she inserted her credit card to pay for the eggs and oil she'd come for and the tin of lemon shortbread she hadn't.

Ten minutes later, outside her first-floor rental on a steep curve of the port city's longest road, she reached into her bag again for her keys. And, standing in front of her door, felt everything plummet inside her as if she'd just stepped into the empty shaft of an elevator.

It was back, bunched up again inside her bag. The same worn

black cotton and white pulse line. The same eerily familiar open neck. She was certain she'd handed it off to the cashier.

And then, perhaps because she had once risked her life in a similar garment and still regarded that time as the pivotal aspect of who she was, she lifted the sweater over her head and pulled it on.

Olga was sweeping stray bits of marijuana leaves off the floor of her bookstore when her friend Lena called, panicking about something having to do with a sweater. Hold on, Olga said into her cordless phone, I can't hear you. I'm back in Poetry. Her reception was far better up in Conspiracy, near the front windows. She could hear clearly enough at the register, too, where she rang up the occasional book—and, yes, also sold a formidable amount of weed.

Of course, I know it doesn't make sense, Lena said with the declarative tone of her generation. I opened my tote bag and it was back, which I know is impossible, but here it is.

I think you're reading too much Saramago, Olga said as she pushed open the front door and stepped outside. What you need to do is sit down with a cup of tea and read someone who doesn't stray so much from reality, someone like—

It's hers, Lena interrupted. I knew something about the sweater was familiar. I just looked up Maria P.'s obituary. She has it on in the photo. Or, no, maybe it's more of a check mark on her sweater, but still.

On whose sweater?

In front of the store now, Olga bent down despite the stiff protest of her knees to remove an empty bag of potato chips someone had tossed in her tulips. She didn't see why, just because she used a claw-footed bathtub for a flower bed, she should be subjected to more trash than anyone else on the hill.

Today, however, there was rampant rubbish for everyone. A scattering of run-over cabbage leaves had formed a grimy pattern across the width of the street. In her exile years, Olga had missed what the love of her life had called the accidental garbage art up this high in the hills above the port, where the city rarely sent anyone to clean the streets. Along the opposite curb, someone had tossed what looked like a full carton of milk, the splattered liquid now trickling gritty and increasingly gray down the hill, forming rather lovely squares around the cobblestones.

Are you listening? Lena asked on the phone. Did you fix your internet? You have to look up the obituary for Maria P. She's the student I told you I kept seeing in photos with Victor at the tuition marches. The way she was beaming at him at the podium, Olga, I had a sick feeling. I know he pushed her in front of that bus, Lena said—her declarations coming faster now—I'm certain of it.

Oh stop, you're not certain, Olga said, reminding Lena how many people got run over by buses barreling down the hills toward the port all the time. Maybe the girl was talking on one of those stupid new cellular phones, Olga said, and forgot to look up the road.

Maria was on a presidential fellowship, Lena said, and in civil engineering. That's not a person who would absentmindedly step in front of a diesel bus she could hear rumbling toward her from a block away.

Unless she was drunk, Olga said.

But Lena was no longer listening. She had already spun too far up into the tornado of her own conclusions. In a lower, more determined voice Lena declared Maria must have sent the sweater from some kind of afterlife limbo, the closest sweater Maria could find to her own. The design is a little different, Lena went on, but what else could a sweater that similar mean? Maria must be stuck in some kind of way station for murder victims and found out there what I let Victor get away with. Maybe she'll be stuck in a limbo state until I do something.

Olga tried to point out that Lena was projecting a considerable amount of meaning onto a sweater that could just be an odd coincidence. It's possible, Olga said, the cashier didn't want to bother with the Lost and Found on her meager five-minute break and decided to just slip it back in your bag.

But what about the obituary? Lena's voice rose again. I have the photo open on my computer, Olga—the sweater has the same open neckline and the check mark on the front is practically a zigzag. It's from her, I'm certain of it. And I could go to the police right now. I drank at the Minnow in my student days. I know that curve on Trinity Hill where she was killed. I could describe it, how I was walking up Trinity that night and saw Victor push her in front of that bus.

Except you didn't see him do that, Olga pointed out, insisting Lena come up to the bookstore to talk this through. You just have a hunch, Olga reminded her, and he has the backing of the entire Truth and Justice Party.

A week after a bus ran over a certain student activist on Trinity Hill, a prominent young senator by the name of Victor turned to the woman beside him in bed and made an offer. Through her ninth-floor windows, the view was pure blue, a few cruise ships moving along the divide between water and sky. There were no other buildings erected as flush against the ocean as this one. It jutted out farther on the rocks than any of the other high-rises on this coveted coastline north of the port. The first time he'd slept here, months ago, had been partially out of curiosity. He'd wanted to know what it would be like to have his way with a woman who possessed such an exceptional view.

Waking each day to a horizon this continuous, he thought, could change the way a man approached things. Especially waking beside a woman who'd grown up among the founders of the TJP who still controlled the party—and therefore nearly every district on the island—since Cato. And he needed to do something to put an end to any rumors that might be circulating in the Senate behind his back, or among Maria's friends. She had assured him she'd told no one about her trips to his apartment, but she was a girl, and girls were feline, always purring up to one another with their secrets.

Marriage hadn't occurred to him as a potential solution until this morning. However, until this morning he had never lingered quite as long beside this meticulously maintained woman and her singular view. The handful of times he'd slept with her last summer, he'd lost interest too quickly in what she had to say to stick around after he woke. He preferred women with more ideas of their own, ideas they were hungry for him to hear and respond to—he relished being the one to dispense the sentence or two of affirmation they were after, and gauge what might happen after that.

But he'd been careful not to let the door shut with a woman this connected. He'd continued to call every few weeks and tell her he was just too overwhelmed to come by and see her—which had been true. He hadn't seen much of anyone. Except for the afternoons he took off to wait in his apartment for Maria to arrive with her latest scribbled calculations for eliminating tuition.

I hope it's obvious that I'm falling in love with you, he said to the woman as he watched her draw up her smooth, toned legs and smile. In fact, he continued, I'm wondering what you might say if I proposed right now.

On one condition, she replied, and Victor braced himself for an inquiry, a promise that he'd had no more than passing contact with that student who'd introduced him several times at the marches, the one killed last week above the Minnow.

But the woman's only condition was that he promise to always speak well of her father.

Victor propped his head on his hand to consider her more closely. Her robust chin was at odds with her thin face, and her augmented breasts, alluring as they were, looked out of sync with the otherwise blunt angles of her body. She'd made a far more striking impression coming toward him at the cocktail party where they'd first met than she did up this close in bed. The event had been for one of the most influential senators in the TJP. Victor had been standing alone by the windows, probing his teeth with the trio of toothpicks he'd accumulated from the lobster balls, when a trim woman in a strapless dress approached him, her smile as promising yet unquantifiable as the locked contents of a jewel box. She'd introduced herself as the senator's eldest daughter. Cristina, she'd added, as if it were an afterthought.

Under the sheets with him now, Cristina drew a little closer. In bed with me, she said, you can criticize my father all you want—just never in public.

Victor extended his hand and made much ado of tucking a lock of her lightened hair behind her ear. Together, he said, I think we could really wake up this sedated island.

Oh, I think we will. Cristina gave a playful bite to his shoulder, after which Victor mounted her more tenderly than he'd mounted any woman in years. For it was clear now she was going to marry him regardless. He didn't have to accept her one condition, and she wasn't going to inquire about Maria P.

In lieu of performing a Google search, Olga was rolling a robust joint for her friend. She hadn't gotten around to fixing her internet—or the plumbing for that matter. What for? She felt lighter inside when she deliberately streamlined her requirements of the world. The less she needed, the less guilty she felt about continuing to exist while the love of her life had not. When she needed to relieve herself, she forced her reluctant knees to deliver her out the back door of the bookstore and down the crumbling stairwell to her abode in the row of homes below.

If her neighbors living along the same staircase glimpsed her gray head bobbing slowly by and guessed she was headed home to relieve her bowels again, well, that was their problem. They already had some idea of what soldiers had done to her. Everyone in walking distance of the bookstore knew some rumored version of what she must have endured at the outset of the regime, when she'd been rounded up with hundreds of other student protesters. Although what had been done to the love of her life, right in front of her, was known to no one.

Her mythical status as one of the few exiles who'd returned to the island had even found its way into various travel guides, which caused a trickle of young backpackers from the northern country that had hosted her. The backpackers shuffled into the store greasy-haired and eager to convey what they'd learned in college about their government's insidious meddling in the rigged election that put Cato in power—as if any of it might be news to Olga. As if she might not be aware that their secret service had supplied the weapons and created the media panic about a Communist Threat that had barely existed.

It was for these earnest-faced young northerners that Olga had put together the Conspiracy section under the front window. She kept it stocked with the crumbling leather-bound volumes of Trotsky and Marx that people continued to find buried in their backyards when they dug a hole for a dead dog or to uproot some unwanted shrub. Owning such books now didn't mean much of anything, which was why people in the hills kept selling her their disinterred editions of Lenin's *The State and Revolution* for less than the cost of a pack of cigarettes. Olga then sold the editions for triple that to her eager young northerners as souvenirs.

A few days earlier, she'd had an unusual northerner come in, a fellow in his midthirties so freshly bathed he still smelled of soap and asking if she carried poetry. Even odder, he'd pulled a scone for her out of his bag from some baking he'd done that morning in his hostel, a situation so unexpected, and delicious, she'd reported it to Lena.

Most hours, when she had any customers at all—either for cannabis or literature—they were from the new liberal arts college up the hill. She had initially been put off by the righteous air of its young professors who'd taken part in the marches to get rid of Cato, especially Lena, whose haughty enunciation had immediately given her away as hailing from a conservative private school up the coast.

Olga had assumed Lena wouldn't last any longer instructing college students to become municipal teachers than the four years Lena herself had lasted teaching in the municipal system before she scurried back to the calm of university lecture halls. Olga had assumed it wouldn't be long before Lena, with her pretty face and commendable ass, would get married to some classmate from her private-school days and move into a beachfront high-rise with a doorman.

But six years later, Lena was still scribbling long notes on her students' responses to Freire's *Pedagogy of the Oppressed*, still objecting when the head of her department jokingly called her and the other young female instructors his harem. There was an indomitable ferocity to Lena that Olga had not expected and had come not only to admire but to count on to recharge her own. And so it was with genuine concern and the deepest affection that Olga was now rolling the fattest possible joint for her friend.

She hoped a little weed would subdue Lena long enough to realize this sweater was simply an enticing coincidence. Olga had pursued a ghost once herself, a man who sat down across from her on a bus a few months into her exile years. He'd had the same splotchy pigment across the back of his hands as the soldier who'd brought food into the room where she and the love of her life had been detained. The man on the bus looked slightly older but with the same round face and conflicted expression, though Olga was certain that soldier couldn't be alive. She'd heard his voice outside the room defying an order. After his objection, she'd heard the blast of a bullet and he'd never entered again.

Yet there he was on the bus, in front of her, and she convinced herself he must be an apparition come to find her in the vast inhospitable country where she'd experienced such loneliness she'd begun to feel like a specter as well. When the man rose to exit the bus, she knew she wouldn't be able to live with herself if she didn't follow him and see if he had appeared to reveal some kind of message, to convey that the love of her life was not dead but still breathing in some secret cell in the interior.

Even before the man abruptly turned and came at her with the knife, she had known it was just an uncanny resemblance, that she was trailing him because trauma made a kite of the mind and there was no telling what kind of wind might take hold of it.

Lena hailed one of the island's shared cabs to get up the hill to the bookstore faster. A pair of beak-nosed elderly women in the backseat who looked like sisters slid over to make room for her. As Lena crammed in next to them, the sisters smiled at her as if she were a child. She wondered what expression would come over their faces if she told them she was wearing the sweater of the student who'd been murdered last week by the port district's much celebrated young senator.

But what would come of saying such a thing to a pair of elderly sisters in a shared cab?

And so Lena gave the sisters what they were expecting: the docile smile of a teacher who taught first-year pedagogy students in a marginal college, a woman given a name almost as common on the island as Maria. When Lena had confessed to Victor the implicit expectation she felt to be as ordinary and predictable as her name, he'd said what about Helen of Troy—nothing predictable about starting the Trojan War, right? He'd suggested she think of herself as Helen's descendant, instigating the end of her island's regime one flaming police car at a time. All it would take, he told her, was a little gasoline in a bottle.

They'd been sitting on the plaid couch in Victor's basement at the time. She'd been in her second term at the university, Victor in his third in political science and revered by everyone in the movement. She'd known that his interest in her had been the only reason she'd been included among the students secretly organizing the marches. At the meetings, everyone deferred to him. He'd deliver his ideas with such precision and hypnotic confidence that he left them all mesmerized. When any of them presented an idea, they'd turn to Victor for validation. If he nodded in agreement, others began to nod, too.

Riding now in the cab, Lena couldn't remember if Victor had first kissed her on the sofa then, or if it had been later, after she'd made her first Molotov cocktail in the shed behind his house. For hours afterward she'd felt dizzy from the gas fumes but also from the audacity of what they were doing. If they didn't die, it was entirely possible they might usher in the country's first legitimate election in over a decade.

Soak the rag a little more, Victor had urged her. Get it good and drenched.

Victor woke and for a moment didn't recognize the woman playing with his inner leg hair and arguing in such a strained voice on her phone. Father, it just feels right, the woman was saying. I'm engaged to him now and that's it.

Victor twitched as the details reassembled. When he drew his leg away, Cristina made a motion with her tongue as if she were a python. There was nothing like a little sleep to reveal to a man how much panic was shaping his perceptions. But whether this naked woman intended to constrict him to death or not, she had just said "engaged" while on the phone with the head of the Senate Transparency Committee, and there was no backing out now.

As Victor had done at every moment of remorse or shame in the past decade, he blamed Lena. If she hadn't made such an idiotic mistake, he never would have ended up with his hands around her neck. When she lost consciousness and slumped to the ground like a sack of apples, he hadn't been able to breathe himself.

Oh, it was astounding how low, low, low a single lapse of self-control could sink a man, convincing him of something sick in his nature. But he'd never lost control again, not the way he had with Lena.

Or not, that is, until Maria.

Beside him, Cristina hung up the phone and cupped his face with her fragrant, just-moisturized hands. Was I too loud? I'm sorry. I didn't mean to yank you out of your sleep.

Transaction Log for Olga's
SEEK THE SUBLIME OR DIE

September 6th

10:05, Kundera Report
Dear S, just sold another *Unbearable Lightness* to a student with curls as thick and self-determined as yours. If you'd lived till Kundera came out in translation here, I'm sure you would have known why his books are like cocaine for the undergrad mind.

10:52, New Customer
A reporter named Simon shuffled in, but only for cannabis. He writes about corruption and has a severe stutter you would find endearing. He's just moved back in with his mother up the street and he talked at me as if I were his mother, too, but I enjoyed him anyhow. He told me a stutter is like grief and can never be overcome entirely, no matter how many tactics a person might learn to suppress it.

I said your name aloud, S, after Simon left. I can't remember the last time I said your name anywhere but in my head. You have become my unutterable divine. My mother had her never-spoken-of God she mumbled to when she thought no one was listening, and you are mine.

11:05, Dread
I may be about to fail another friend, S, as I failed you.

Right here, thank you, Lena spoke up from the backseat as they reached the narrow street below Olga's Sublime. The morning clouds were still low and thick over the port, the rundown homes stacked into the hillside still drained of color. The dense fog off the ocean usually retreated by noon, but it had hung on today, muting even the brightest pinks and yellows of the paint chipping off the doors and window frames of the street below Olga's. Once the sun emerged, the port city looked less like a soiled and forgotten heap of laundry. The graffiti on the stairwells, the brightly painted doors, even the rusted tin of the roofs came defiantly alive in the sunlight.

Lena had felt more defiantly alive herself once she'd moved here and definitively left her parents' sealed-off existence. She loved living above the streets she'd marched down as a student, shouting until her throat felt blowtorched. She knew everyone assumed her family, as owners of one of the largest juice factories on the island, had supported the regime—and they weren't wrong. Her grandfather had hired only workers who professed to support Cato. Throughout her childhood, her grandfather had repeated the same justifications for the roundups that everyone in their world of gated homes had, insisting the numbers of people detained and killed were wildly exaggerated.

Although at night, as a teenager, through the wall her room shared with her father's study, she'd heard him listening to what the foreign stations were reporting about the island. Her father never brought up what he heard, and Lena never told him how many nights she'd stayed awake, straining to make out what the voices on the radio were saying about all the police shootings that went unmentioned in the island's newspapers.

She'd also never told her parents or brothers about her increasing involvement with either the protests or with Victor. To explain her ever more frequent overnight absences, she'd invented sleepovers to study with girlfriends. One evening as she packed her bag, she'd looked up and found her father in the doorway of her room. She'd thought he was going to confront her, but he'd just remained there with a pained expression, watching her. She'd kissed him and assured him she was meeting up with friends who looked out for her and that she would be fine.

An hour later, at the meeting, Victor had announced to everyone that she'd be in charge of flyers for the next march, and it had felt like a baptism. She drafted each one as if it were destined for a museum. She ran her fingers twice over each fold while Victor paced and strategized in his basement. They began to repeat the ritual several nights a week, Victor thinking out loud, Lena murmuring in agreement as she went on folding and folding, determined to prove she was as committed and relentless as he was. They'd talked endless times about the unfairness of it, how the police wouldn't dare beat her if they caught her. When Victor told her she needed to be more brazen at the marches, to remember that her family could get her released with no more than a phone call, she had nodded and said of course, had begun throwing more Molotovs than all of the other girls combined.

The day she misplaced the draft of the flyer had been after a night staying up together until four a.m. She'd felt nauseous with exhaustion by the time they got to campus. The draft contained all the information for the next march and she hadn't intended to take it with her. They all knew agents for the government were crawling like ants through every trash can on campus. She'd checked her books and her bag over and over before she'd gone to Victor's to see if she'd left the draft of the flyer in his basement.

Moving up the steep stairwell to Olga's back door, Lena could still recall the splatter of Victor's spit on her face after she told him she didn't know where she'd misplaced it. When he pushed her against the wall and grabbed her throat, she'd thought he was just panicking for a second. But then he'd smashed his palm over her nostrils. He'd shouted about her father and grandfather, yelled they were the reason she was so careless and couldn't be trusted with anything. Each time she'd managed to gasp for air, she'd apologized again, but Victor had just clamped his hand down, harder.

More than ten years later, the thought of those seconds before she'd blacked out in his basement still caused her lungs to stiffen, the memory of her nose crushed under his palm still startling enough to suck all the other contents out of her mind. Reaching the back door of the Sublime, she didn't know if she was out of breath from the steepness of the steps or from what was replaying in her head.

Finally! Olga called from the front of the store. I have a gift for you.

I need some water first. Lena kissed her friend on the cheek and picked up the plastic bottle Olga refilled each morning at home. Lena had offered once to help her pay for the pipes to be fixed, but Olga had given her a vicious stare and said if she was looking for a corporate sponsor, she'd let her know.

That sweater looks good on you. Olga held out the joint to her. You should order clothes from the afterlife more often.

Lena frowned at this, inhaling as Olga let out a stoned, gravelly laugh, her body as imposing as a king's in the large stained velvet armchair she kept behind the register. Olga was broad shouldered and big boned, her gray hair chopped short as a man's. Even high, she had an intimidating air, and Lena didn't mention the computer monitor sitting on the floor until Olga motioned to it.

Internet's still down, Olga said.

I see that, Lena replied. I should have printed the obituary so you could see it's practically the same sweater. I know Victor pushed her in front of that bus, and he isn't going to get away with it. With Olga's tenacious gaze on her, the words felt less convincing in her mouth than they had when she'd declared them on the phone, alone in her living room. She felt the granules of conviction she'd stirred up at her computer already dissolving inside her.

When Olga asked if she was over her crazy idea yet of concocting a story for the police, Lena pivoted toward the wall.

You know Victor will use your grandfather to discredit anything you claim, Olga said. I bet he'll go after your whole family. He'll get his minions calling for a boycott of every juice coming out of that factory.

Olga motioned for the joint and Lena wordlessly returned it to her. Of course Victor would do that. She had confessed her grand-father's hiring practices to him as if he were the head priest in the church of reprehensible complicity. Just last week there had been a big story in the news about a right-wing family in the interior that no one had exposed before, a family that had stored arms on their horse farm for the regime. People were tired of rehashing the same familiar cast of villains from the Cato years. They were hungry for other wealthy families who had yet to own up to their share of the blame. Victor could easily make hers the next.

With a quiet huff of defeat, Lena looked down at the white pulse line across her chest, how precisely the zigzag fell at the rise of her breasts, how perfectly her body complied with the design.

Victor and I joked about having a baby and naming her Futura, she told Olga. We were going to take Futura with us when we went to vote.

Olga whistled. Can you imagine if you'd had a Futura with that sociopath?

Lena let her head fall back. Even if she had more evidence than a sweater sent from the afterlife, her accusations would lead to noth-ing. No one would take her claims seriously. She'd be dismissed on the radio as some bitter ex-girlfriend who'd grown up with maids tying her shoes, a woman raised in one of those sickening families that still wouldn't use the word *regime*.

When she'd ranted on the phone with Olga, it had felt possible to postpone the consideration of how easily Victor would make her a pariah. With his cult status on campus, he'd have no problem getting her fired. Her family could lose the factory. They might have to leave the island. Victor wouldn't just burn up her life, he'd incinerate that of her brothers and their wives, her nephews and little niece who'd just started school.

Until Olga said it, it hadn't occurred to her that the cashier could have been the one who returned the sweater to her bag. It seemed unlikely—but no less so than being haunted.

She squinted up at the water spots extending across the ceiling. She followed the edge of the largest one, its faint yet relentless advance above her head.

Victor told his fiancée he was headed to his office, which would be true eventually. He needed some air off the sea first. Since college, he'd liked to walk the docks along the port, to process things while moving between the cargo ships. It cleared his mind to drift between the giant stacks of containers, the men shouting at each other as they operated the cranes.

Today, however, something wasn't right. The first dock was full of people who didn't belong there. Women and teenagers. Doddering old men with binoculars.

What the hell's going on? he asked a man who was crouching, about to secure a rope to the dock.

Whales, the man answered. A pair of them, mating.

Where? Victor looked out at the ocean, which was a dull color today, the clouds round and gray and piled like potatoes.

Hard to guess, the man said. They might be going at it down there right now. All anyone's seen is their backs but people keep showing up. The kiosk's been out of cigarettes for days.

He turned his face toward Victor with this last piece of information and Victor noticed the man's right eye wasn't tracking in sync with the left one. Victor backed away. He wasn't up to dealing with any peculiar faces right now, and no fucking whales.

He gave the man the briefest of nods and continued down the dock, moving past a cluster of teenage boys eating chocolate bars and laughing. But seriously, one of them said, how big do you think a whale's boner is?

And then the boys laughed harder and Victor felt a rush of revulsion at their predictable humor and pimpled faces. And revulsion, too, at the thought of his own face, so distant now from a boy's face. He'd felt painfully old and lonely when his younger brother began questioning him over lunch on Sunday. It had been excruciating to stiffen and deny Freddy an answer, to will a growing distance from his only brother. But Freddy had been relentless. You must know something, Freddy had insisted, you slept with her. Was she a drunk? Was she reckless? How did she end up in front of that bus?

Olga aimed to save her secret stash of whiskey for special occasions. But if a friend convinced of having received a garment from the afterlife wasn't such an occasion, then what was? Marijuana alone hadn't been enough to get Lena to take the zigzag sweater off. With the faucet out of commission, there'd been no way to rinse her shot glasses. Instead, they finished the whiskey sailor-style, straight from the bottle. Lena still had the sweater on, but at least she was horizontal in it now, sprawled and tipsy on the busted couch in Conspiracy.

By the time the whiskey was gone, the morning had taken on the improvisational feel of evening and Olga suggested they pull out the fake beards Lena had brought for her last birthday. Lena had shown up for the party with ten cotton-ball Santa beards trimmed and painted gray in honor of Olga's legendary impersonations of a certain bearded revolutionary mythologized in movies produced by the same northerners who'd had him killed. When she'd opened the box, Olga had nearly cried from delight at the sight of those beards.

By the end of the party, most of the elastic bands had snapped and broken. But a few of the beards still had their bands intact, and on evenings when she was tipsy enough, she'd cajole friends who came by the store to put them on and play Bearded Revolutionaries with her.

You ready, comrade? Olga waved one at Lena now.

Oh, I can't, it's not even noon. One of my students might walk in.

But Olga had already snapped on a beard and was adjusting the elastic. Come on, she said. The time for revolution is now!

Olga launched her large body out of her velvet chair. People, she declared, have to know they will not face mere boys this time. People have to know this time they will face bearded women!

She stumbled over to her friend. Get up, comrade. It may not seem yet like we've entered the millennium of bearded women, but this one's ours, I'm telling you. The millennium of bearded book vendors has arrived!

You're crazy, Lena said, her words slurred from the whiskey. But she didn't resist when Olga leaned over and slipped a beard's elastic band over her head. Soon, they were both up and shouting over each other about justice and a beard-for-everyone movement that would spread from bookstores to revolutionary all-night libraries. To cover the electricity, they'd sell the city's best marijuana and coffee. They'd sell beards in every size—little ones for kids and discount beards for retirees who binged on murder mysteries.

Olga grabbed one of the 1970 leather-bound copies of Marx's *The Communist Manifesto* on display in the Conspiracy section and held it up to her ear like a phone. Karl, we've got some news for you boys. There will be no true revolution until there are beards covering every chin in every nation!

That's right, Lena said, reaching down for a crumbling edition of Simone Weil's *On the Abolition of All Political Parties*. Simone, dear, we have not given up! Lena declared, frayed cotton balls flapping against her face as she whipped around.

Olga punched her fist at the air and scanned the shelf for who else they might summon for their midday manifesto when she heard a voice saying her name with the thick accent of a northerner. She spun around to find Oscar in the doorway, the blond-as-butter baker who had come in Tuesday with the scones.

Well, well, she said, look who's come to join the revolution.

Revolution was not what Oscar had in mind when he walked into Olga's Seek the Sublime or Die.

It was her side enterprise, and perhaps some more poetry.

Although this morning the main reason he'd come by was to give Olga the croissants he'd made for her as a thank you. Earlier in the week, he'd mentioned a Yeats poem to her that he'd been obsessed with in college and she had rummaged through a dozen stacks for an anthology she'd acquired years ago from another northerner. The anthology had indeed contained the Yeats poem, on a wrinkled page covered with water stains and someone else's pencil marks. Still, the lines were as luminous as Oscar remembered them from the undergrad poetry seminar he'd taken before dropping out to go to culinary school.

He'd gotten disillusioned with culinary school as well. Then with the vegan bakery he'd worked in after that.

After nine years burning out in one job and city after another, endlessly dissatisfied, convinced there must be somewhere that would suit him better, he'd received a small inheritance from his step-grandmother and decided to blow the money on an extended wander in the cheaper countries south of his own.

Or at least he had been wandering, until a bargain flight to the island had delivered him into the dilapidated bohemian labyrinth of this port city, and he'd gone no further. Its bright, joyful disorder felt so in sync with his own hapless internal state that he'd rented a room for a month in a hostel with a decent kitchen. He'd signed up for some cheap language classes to better grasp what was going on—how to reply, for example, when two drunk women in what looked like painted Santa beards asked if he'd come to join their revolution.

I don't know if I came for that, he said in their language.

Oh, I think you did, comrade. Olga slapped him on the back and turned to her friend. This is the wandering baker I told you about, who came in with the scones and bought that anthology I've been trying to unload for a hundred years.

Her friend had yanked off her beard as soon as Oscar walked in. She was shorter and a good twenty years younger than Olga, who was nearly his own height and broader in the shoulders than he was. Next to Olga, her friend looked somewhat childlike. She had a delicate, chiseled face but there was something ferocious about her, too—a scrutiny of the world so intense it bordered on sensual. He blushed as he watched her take in the batik pants he'd bought the week before at an artisan fair and his faded, decade-old T-shirt from college.

This Place Is Gorges, she said, reading the front of his shirt out loud. Is that supposed to be funny? Doesn't gorge mean a deep divide?

Oscar nodded and, in halting, nervous sentences, tried to explain about the other "gorgeous" in his language, which meant beautiful, his freckles heating on his face.

Gorges and gorgeous—there's a word for that corny kind of joke in your country, isn't there? A pun, right? I certainly got an overload of those living with you people. Puns, and guns! Olga shouted in his language, lurching drunkenly in his direction. That pretty much sums up your nation, wouldn't you say, Oscar—puns and guns? But more than puns, what would really give this revolution a boost would be some of those scones of yours.

Would croissants do? Oscar pulled them out, still warm inside the paper towels he'd wrapped around them in his hostel. I made them to thank you for the anthology.

I believe these will do just fine. Olga snatched two and tried to press one into her friend's palm, but the friend yanked her hand away and made a face.

Oh stop it, Lena. You know you're ravenous, Olga said. Just put it in your mouth. Oscar here's a professional, aren't you? Olga winked at him and Oscar nodded though he wasn't entirely sure what she was winking about.

What he did know with certainty was that all the filaments in his brain skittered into the word YES when Olga's friend reluctantly bit into his croissant. When she licked a flake off her lip, he thought Byzantium. He was entering the poem, had reencountered its lines here for a reason. He'd finally reached the elusive season it described, the one after disillusionment, after prolonging his youth until he had become its aging narrator, drifting like an ancient, paltry thing, no more than a coat on a stick—

> And therefore I have sailed the seas and come
> To the holy city of Byzantium.

Transaction Log for Olga's
SEEK THE SUBLIME OR DIE

Still Thursday, S, but had to fill you in on this curious abundance of an afternoon!

12:35, Received
No books but some pretty excellent croissants from my new baker friend with the shaggy hair. For a northerner, he seems like a humble, decent chap. I may have to coax Lena to take him home, but I could tell she wanted to. What famous poet is it who said distraction can crack open unexpected doors?

5:09, Just Bought
An entire wheelbarrow full of books. Twenty-six of them, buried since your last year on this earth, S. A twelve-year-old from up the street who'd never come into the store before wheeled them down. He'd hit upon the books while digging a hole to bury his pet bird. Here's what I got for the cost of a pizza—he was hoping for more, but aren't we all:

-2 volumes of Marx

-1 leather-bound *Remembrance of Things Past*, although Proust never sells, a fact that led to a pleasant discussion with the kid about why so many people buried their Prousts, whether it came from a fear of appearing to sympathize with the French Revolution, or if it had more to do with the fact that Proust is long-winded and hard to follow, which we tend to associate with intellectuals and communists. The kid laughed at this and told me he read a long book once at school and liked it. I told him that probably means he's a communist at heart. He laughed like it was the funniest thing he'd ever heard. To be a communist, S, is nothing but a punch line in this country now.

-And the one great find in the kid's wheelbarrow, great enough to cause a flutter in my ever more corrupt and capitalistic heart: an illustrated *Kama Sutra*. I placed it immediately in the front window.

Sad prediction for the future
The *Sutra* will go to a professor who has sex with no one.

Lena had been determined to find Oscar's croissant a tasteless failure—
bland as the blockbusters of his country.

But the hint of salt, the way the layers flaked and dissolved on
her tongue—everything about Oscar's damn croissant was undeni-
ably satisfying.

Hours later, she could still taste it in her mouth when she woke
in her bedroom. She'd intended to take a short nap to sleep off the
whiskey before resuming her Google search on Maria P. But it was
dark by the time she woke, her room drafty from the damp air that
pressed in every evening from the ocean.

Still dizzy from the whiskey, she slid off her bed. The floor felt
liquid-cold. With a shiver, she stopped at her dresser for a pair of
socks from the wide top drawer where she also kept her underwear and bras. She sorted them into three orderly sections as her
family's help had done, which made the unexpected object now
in the left front corner immediately apparent. Folded neatly upon
itself was a lacy, padded white satin bra—the fussily ornate kind
a mother bought for her teenaged daughter, or that a naïve,
eager-to-please girl in college might continue wearing to please a
boyfriend, its lace-covered satin so stiff and immaculate it shim-
mered.

She flicked on the light to make sure she wasn't mistaken, was
indeed awake and not trapped in some kind of whiskey-induced
dream state. But with the light on, the fact of the bra there in her
drawer became indisputable. Tucked into the corner next to the beige

cotton bras she wore until the clasps broke was a bright white intruder that unspooled something inside her.

She'd been wearing such a bra the first time Victor had seen her undressed in full daylight. They'd gone in her mother's car to a little beach cove up the coast. As they'd climbed over the rocks to the hidden sandbar below, Victor told her that the previous evening his father had run into someone at a bar who'd been with Victor's uncle the night he'd been detained. For over a decade, Victor's father had been trying to find out what had happened to his brother Edgar, who'd been among the schoolteachers rounded up for protesting against the bogus election results declaring Cato the new president. Victor's father had never stopped asking and searching on the chance that Edgar might still be imprisoned somewhere on the island. But the man at the bar said he'd seen Edgar shot and loaded onto a truck.

As Lena had listened, she'd thought of her family, her mother floating that same morning in their enormous pool, of her grandfather lowering his newspaper just last Sunday and declaring that the damn communists had gotten what they deserved. She'd felt nauseous with guilt as she'd stood beside Victor, watching the thin strands of kelp slapping back and forth against the rocks. She hadn't known what else to say beyond sorry, then apologize for repeating such an inadequate response.

When Victor hooked his fingers under the hem of her shirt, she'd helped him lift it over her head, eager to make of her body a deeper, further apology. The stiff white satin of her bra had taken on an eerie sheen in the sunlight as he pulled her straps down and slid it to her waist. She'd felt irremediably naked watching him take in her breasts and the rest of her on the uneven slope of sand beneath them, as if no clothes would ever entirely conceal her from anyone again.

In her bedroom, staring down at the white satin bra folded upon itself in the corner of her drawer, she felt the shock all over again of Victor's bitten nail, the raw scrape of it that morning when he shoved his finger upward, inside her.

Just shut the drawer, she told herself. But she'd come to trust her impulse for self-recrimination more than any other.

And so her hand made its way to the bra.

And alone in her cold bedroom, she hooked it on.

Sealed behind the heavy door of his office, Victor lifted the day's newspaper until it formed a barricade around his face. He never read the Arts section unless there was something in it about his brother and even then he rarely finished a column. They'd run a whole interview with Freddy this time about his new play opening tonight. Victor pulled the paper a little closer with the intention of forcing himself to read at least some of it. But the photograph was too distracting. He didn't understand why Freddy had to dress to such an extreme for a publicity shot, wrapping his neck in a sparkling velvet scarf as if he were some corpulent opera star.

I'm assuming all the characters will be gay in this one, too, he'd said when Freddy told him about the interview, to which Freddy responded with one of his booming laughs. In grade school, Victor had felt conspicuous about his inability to laugh as fully, or freely, as his brother could. But once he realized the respect his seriousness generated in others, he was glad for Freddy to be the funny one, for his brother's inimitable laugh to occasionally ease something in him as well.

As often as he could, he tried to make it to Freddy's openings, although he'd missed the last one to be with Maria. Her family had gone away for the night, and she'd asked him to come to her this time. Until he'd entered her bedroom, with its girlish purple-trimmed curtains, he'd resisted thinking about how much younger she was, how disgusted her parents would be if they knew. The narrowness of Maria's single mattress, the sight of her nightgown folded under her pillow, all of it had hurled him back to Lena.

The second he saw Maria folding flyers, arguing with some other girls, the similarity had pierced him. Maria was much taller, her face longer. But she had a similar way of squinting when she made a point, that same intensity that made other girls shrink a little, away from her.

But there had been more than that as well, something about Maria's oversized sweaters, her habit of tugging at the sleeves, as if she didn't trust herself to ever get them positioned exactly right. Her unease with her body had made his mouth dry, breaking down whatever it was in a man's mind that kept his longings separate from his regrets.

There's just something about this Maria, he'd told Freddy when he apologized for missing the last opening, I couldn't say no.

At that point, Maria had been working mainly on emails and posters, the details girls always liked to do. He'd mentioned her name to his brother without even thinking about it.

He hadn't expected her to get so adamant, so overcome with manic ambition. When Maria showed him the elaborate strategy she'd written up for how the country might fully finance tuition for the poorest students on the island, he'd flattered her. Any number of similar plans had been circulating in the Senate for years. But he hadn't seen any harm in encouraging her, in exaggerating how innovative he found her thinking as he slipped her shirt down off her shoulder. He'd told her she was really on to something, and Maria had kept chattering, breathless and excited by his approval—all of it so familiar that he hadn't realized he'd begun to murmur Lena's name until Maria pushed him off her.

Victor tensed, felt a cramp in his thigh. He had to stop rethinking how it all had unfolded. The night doorman at his building hardly looked up from the soccer on his TV when someone entered, and how many times, total, had Maria come to his apartment? Ten? Twelve? Maybe even less than that.

Victor hit the button on his phone for his secretary and asked her to order a crate of wine for the Zodiac, for it to be delivered to the theater by six. Expense it as civic engagement, please, he added.

Most of the artsy types who filled the Zodiac didn't bother to vote but they were talkers. He could bring Cristina and use it to make their engagement public. The cramped, noisy lobby of the theater would make it impossible for Freddy to get started with any of his questions again. It was a brilliant plan, really. Superb. How many times had he been chased down in the protests and never caught? He was a street dog, always had been. And everyone loved the emergence of a new power couple to follow in the papers.

Victor widened his legs to roll his chair closer to the edge of his desk and phoned his brother. What would you say to your favorite senator sponsoring the wine tonight?

Funny you called, Freddy said. I was just working on something and thinking of you.

SCENES FROM *THE PRUNING* OF A FUTURE PRESIDENTIAL CANDIDATE
(WORK-IN-PROGRESS BY FMG)

At the outset of the regime

SET

A shabby kitchen, paint chipping on the cabinets.

A platter with a roasted chicken reigns, untouched, on a simple table.

The lights come up as the father closes an imaginary door and says good-bye to someone who has already stepped out.

After locking the imaginary door, the father sits and covers his face.

Also at the table:

A plastic doll in a high chair,

A wife in a housedress,

and a man wearing a sign around his neck that says FUTURE CANDIDATE, AGE 5.

MOTHER

They'll release him.

They can't keep all those people locked up indefinitely, and your brother knows everyone.

47

He'll find someone who can—

FATHER

Just stop it, would you please?

What do you know?

You don't know anything.

Pause.

The mother starts to weep, which sets off the baby in the high chair.
As the baby is a doll, its wails emerge from the speakers.

The Future Candidate's lips begin to tremble.
He hunches over to hide it.

At his first all-out sob,
the father grabs his shoulder, forces him to sit up.

FATHER

Don't you start, son.

Keep it in.

Find a spot on the wall like a senator.

Fix your gaze on it.

You want to be a man, right?

The father stares out at the audience, wipes his eyes.

Olga had just begun to sip her morning thermos of tea on Friday when Lena ducked in, jerking the loose door handle harder than necessary. Without a hello or any sort of greeting, Lena parked in front of the register and yanked up her sweatshirt and the tank top underneath it, revealing a white lace bra that looked at least a size too small, trapping in a pair of taut, round breasts even lovelier than Olga had expected.

See this? Lena asked. It appeared in my drawer last night.

Well, my friend, God was good to you. He never left me a bosom that impressive in my drawer. Olga took a rigorous slurp from her thermos.

I meant the bra. Lena blushed and tugged her sweatshirt down. It's hers, Olga. It's Maria P.'s. She's not going to leave me alone until I do something. I haven't owned a bra this lacy and absurd in years. And do you know what the brand name is on the tag? It's Freddy, the brand Freddy! Which also happens to be the name of Victor's brother, right? And Freddy's new show is opening tonight at the Zodiac. It could be another coincidence, I know—Lena held up her hand—but what if it's not? What if Maria wants me to go tonight and ask Freddy whether Victor ever mentioned her? Freddy and I always got along, and maybe Victor himself will show up and I can confront him directly. It's been ten years. It's time, don't you think?

Olga put down her thermos and tried to calmly indicate what a reach this was, to deduce such a convoluted message from a dead stranger based on the tag of a bra, which perhaps had been there in the drawer for years and she just hadn't had a compelling reason to notice it.

But, once again, Lena had wound herself too tightly around her own version to question it. In her adamant, emphatic way, Lena insisted the bra had absolutely not been in her drawer until now, said she was certain it was a second message from Maria.

Olga sighed and lifted her thermos again. She'd been sipping all morning to stay warm and really needed to make a trip down to her house to use the bathroom. Lena yanking up her sweater, the mounting pressure on her bladder, getting pulled again into the consuming rage of crimes without consequences—it was really too much for this early in the morning. She hoped this wasn't going to become a daily phenomenon, Lena rushing in this way, convinced of more garments from the great beyond.

You'll come with me to the play, won't you? Lena leaned forward, bracing her weight over the desk. You said you were sorry you missed Freddy's last play.

I'd be even sorrier if I indulged this concocted logic of yours. Olga took another sip of her tea and immediately regretted it. She squeezed her legs together but it was too late. She closed her eyes. Listen, Lena, I need to close up for a few minutes and go down to the house.

I wish you'd let me fix the pipes for you.

Thank you, Ms. Heiress, but I'm fine taking care of it on my own.

Lena shrunk back from the register and Olga clenched her jaw. A warm drop escaped her. Please, just let me lock up, Lena. I'm sorry, okay? I gave you my opinion yesterday, and you didn't like it. If you want to invoke the wrath of a sociopath because you didn't recognize a bra in your drawer, go ahead. Go and do it. Olga motioned to the door where, through the front window, they both saw Oscar crossing the street, carrying some new treat on a covered plate. He was so eager to reach them he was half loping, his jaunty, bouncing step causing the mop of his blond hair to flap against his forehead.

Well, there's your date for tonight, Olga said. I saw how you looked at him over your croissant.

Transaction Log for Olga's
SEEK THE SUBLIME OR DIE

September 7th

Rough start to the morning, S. Offended Lena, pissed a little in my pants. Only consolation was a decent resale of a book for once:

1:24, Sold
The illustrated *Kama Sutra*, and to the head of Lena's pedagogy department at asking price. Profit margin on horny middle-aged man nobody wants to sleep with:

THREE HUNDRED PERCENT.

It gave me such joy, S, shameless capitalist that I've become!

4:28, Bought
Nothing. Nobody else has come in since Lena's department head, and Lena herself, trusting me enough to lift her shirt like that, to hear out her impossible logic. I didn't mean to be so harsh, S. I just couldn't handle it, how hell-bent she is on self-sabotage, not after forty years scraping away at the same bowl of questions and shame about being forced out of that room and leaving you there, after being so arrogant and naïve, insisting you were paranoid to think you needed to be more careful about the meetings. As if I had any idea what it was like to

live on this island with a last name as obviously Jewish as yours. To have pressured you, after growing up under the cover of a name as common as my father's, with no way for anyone to guess my mother might have gone as a child to the same little synagogue in the South End.

If there is a reason I've lasted, S, I can't fathom what it is.

At the sight of Lena emerging from the bookstore, Oscar nearly dropped his biscuits. The day was not quite as stingy with its light today. A few sunbeams had punctured the thinning clouds, which he hoped was the reason Lena was squinting so intently and not because she was debating whether to acknowledge him. In front of Olga's tub of tulips, she stopped and told him Olga was closing up the Sublime and he couldn't go in.

If he had not seen Lena as recently as yesterday declaring revolution in a beard, or had not been adrift in the world for over a decade and at his most confident among strangers, it is possible the intersection of their lives might have ended there. Or if a produce truck hadn't shuddered up the street just then, propelling a stray zucchini into the air like a lean green quivering bird. Or if they hadn't been united by the wonder of the zucchini passing over their heads before it splattered on the road just beyond them.

I knew it wouldn't be a zucchini that killed me, Oscar said. It's definitely going to be a root vegetable that ends my life.

With only the faintest smile in response, Lena reached over and lifted the foil covering his biscuits. I'm assuming, she said, you were coming to donate these to the revolution.

From the front page of *The Islander*

The young senator, with his ardent eloquence and intense gaze, has become a darling of the age group least likely to vote. "The revolt my generation started ten years ago," he said, "is not even half-finished. What's driven our students into the streets isn't just debt, it's democracy, it's the threat of a return to fascism if only the wealthiest on this island can afford an education."

The senator's swell of youth support has led to predictions of an easy bid for reelection.

As she walked up the hill to campus, Lena found it increasingly hard to breathe in the bra she'd received from the afterlife. She wondered if Maria had intended her to feel this confined and uneasy until she took some kind of action. When she saw the way Maria beamed at Victor in the paper, she should have taken some kind of action, sent a warning. She could have looked up Maria's student email address. And now the girl was under a tombstone at nineteen.

Yes, she absolutely had to go to the Zodiac. Leaving the bookstore, she had no intention of taking Olga's ridiculous advice about bringing Oscar. She loathed the way ogling northerners reduced every meaningful place in the port to a tourist experience. But then there had been the insanity of that flying zucchini, Oscar mentioning death and root vegetables, and suddenly there was sex, which she hadn't had in over a year, coursing as invisibly but indisputably as music between them.

She was still a good five hundred meters from campus but could already hear the drums and shouting of the students. At the corner before the main entrance of the university, she shifted the underwire of the bra one more time though it went on digging into her skin anyway. Outside the front gates, she surveyed the new damage. The protests had begun over the spiraling cost of tuition but had now expanded to the recent release of literacy rates in the interior, which were still as shockingly low as they had been under Cato. In the days since Lena had come by the week before, the students had torn down a stop sign and a pair of streetlights. The mangy stray dogs that lived around the gates were running back and forth, barking at the drums.

Hey, Professor! One of her favorite, feral-haired students called to her from the roof of a rusted Subaru. We just heard the senator's going to do it, he's going to present a free tuition bill to the Senate! Isn't that incredible? He's fucking incredible.

Incredible, Lena repeated before turning her face to the drums.

Victor rubbed his thumb over Cristina's manicured nails, glad he had brought her to the opening, even if the jeans she'd put on were far too new and pressed for the Zodiac crowd. The theater sat at the end of a courtyard. On laundry lines strung between the buildings on either side of the theater, Freddy had suspended several old sheets painted with yet another excessive name for a play. His brother had titled this one *Where He Danced While We Lay Dreaming*, the letters extending across three blue sheets that moved with the breeze as Victor passed beneath them with Cristina.

Inside the Zodiac, the lobby looked even more pitiable and close to collapse than it had at the last show of Freddy's he'd attended. A section of the ceiling tiles was now patched with masking tape. Even scrappier were the now-absent benches in the lobby that had been replaced with two wobbly backseats ripped out of cars. As they turned toward the ticket booth, Cristina pointed at a tall blond northerner. Since when do tourists come to the Zodiac?

Victor saw immediately whom she meant. At the front of the line, the man was fumbling with his money in the slow, exasperating way tourists on the island always seemed to when people were waiting behind them. The small, dark-haired woman beside him turned her head, and Victor felt as if sand had suddenly encrusted his face.

Who is that woman? Cristina asked. She's staring like she knows you.

Just as Oscar bent to retrieve the ticket he'd dropped, the woman behind him stepped on it, pinning the ticket to the ground with the heel of her motorcycle boot. Excuse me, Oscar said from his crouch, but the woman in the boots didn't hear. When he pulled on Lena's sleeve beside him, she didn't react either.

What's going on with the northerner on the floor? he heard someone say off to the left.

Oscar closed his eyes, unsure whether it would be more humiliating to stand up in response or remain crouching a moment longer where he was, waiting for the girl in the motorcycle boot to move her foot. Ashamed at the situation he'd created for himself, he tried to picture his best éclair. A therapist his mother paid for after he quit his vegan bakery job had suggested this strategy for situations that filled him with such a sense of inadequacy he wanted to give up and leave. He'd replayed that éclair so many times in his mind the ingredients now assembled instantaneously: the vanilla bean pods he'd split, the drops of almond extract he'd added to the cream, how capably he'd blended it all into perfection.

And it worked. He opened his eyes and the girl had moved slightly, her boot now only pinning the tip of his ticket. Leaning forward, he managed to retrieve it whole. With a sense of triumph, he rose slowly from the floor, determined to put this minor humiliation behind him. Only Lena was no longer next to him, or anywhere he could spot her nearby. He scanned the crowded lobby. More people kept squeezing inside, none of them as obviously a foreigner as he was. Even upright again like everyone else, he felt conspicuous. Without Lena beside him, he was an intruder here.

A commotion broke out by the far wall and Oscar turned toward the noise. One of the torn-out backseats of a car serving as a bench had tipped over, spilling several people, laughing, onto the floor, but Lena wasn't among them. Oscar had never been in a theater that felt this genuinely precarious and renegade, existing on little more than determination. If he could just find Lena and join her, he could stop feeling so out of place here and savor it. He was still ignoring his mother's questions in her emails, asking what the point of this much wandering at his age could possibly be, why he couldn't at least promise to return by the holidays and start figuring out his life.

At last, he spotted Lena. She was midway through the crowd, slipping ribbon-like between the people continuing to push inside. He realized she must be headed for the bathrooms, had probably tried to tell him but he hadn't heard. But then she stopped and he watched her give a long embrace to a man in an eccentric velvet scarf. It was an embrace that spoke of history, of deep affection, the kind of genuine embrace he'd missed in this year of wandering, and before it in the small city where he'd been living and knew almost no one. Wasn't that the cost, above all, of his habitual dissatisfaction—of having no deeper continuous history with anyone beyond his bitterly divorced parents, and one culinary school friend who'd kept him on her group emails?

With envy, he watched Lena stop again to speak to a couple by the door.

The overhead lights began to blink but Lena ignored them. She ignored whatever Freddy was saying as he trailed behind her toward his brother. Determined not to lose her nerve before she reached Victor, she pushed harder through the crowd. She didn't let herself look away from his stare as she drew closer. His left eye started twitching exactly as it had at meetings for the marches when anyone questioned what he proposed.

Beside him, the smug, heavily made-up plastic decoy of a woman he'd brought along was leaning obliviously against his arm as if he were harmless. And he did look eerily harmless in his gray sweater and jeans. His jawline was not quite as sharp as it had been in college. The skin under his chin was looser, intimations of his mother's second chin beginning to emerge. His posture was still as erect and intimidating, but his stomach wasn't as firm under his sweater. He had a small gut now, the slack body of a bureaucrat who spent his days in an office, and she felt emboldened. Olga had been wrong, or at least about coming here tonight. As a senator, Victor wouldn't dare do anything to her in such a crowded public place. All she would do was say Maria's name and see what came over his face. Or no, she wouldn't say Maria's name. She'd shout it, and loud enough to be certain Freddy and the oblivious woman at Victor's side would have no choice but to hear.

SCENES FROM *THE PRUNING OF A FUTURE PRESIDENTIAL CANDIDATE*
(WORK IN PROGRESS BY FMG)

The present

SET

A crooked poster with the name of a theater.

A few photos from old shows.

Frames can be crooked and hung at random intervals.

CHARACTERS

The ex-girlfriend: flame-like, flickers often, dressed in red.

The fiancée: stiff and icy, dressed in white.

The Future Candidate: muscular, dressed in ridiculous plaids.

The chubby brother: plays accordion, stays out of the way, dressed in velvet.

The lights should come on like an explosion, harsh and all at once.

The chubby brother's first notes of tango should coincide with this explosion.

The characters should shout over it.

EX-GIRLFRIEND

What? You're engaged?

FIANCÉE

Yes, as of yesterday.

We're over the moon.

And you?

How do you know Victor?

EX-GIRLFRIEND

Did you say yesterday?

I guess Maria won't be able to make the wedding, will she?

FIANCÉE

Who?

I'm sorry.

It's so loud in here.

Ex-girlfriend gets up in her face.

EX-GIRLFRIEND

I'm asking about Maria, the stu—

The Future Candidate cuts knifelike between the women.
He makes a violent grab for the ex-girlfriend's wrist.

With cold determination, he twirls her.

His brother, off to the side, spins simultaneously with his accordion.

After the twirl, the notes of the tango are more drawn out.

The Future Presidential Candidate dips the ex-girlfriend.

Mid-dip, she shouts again but no sound comes out.

The onstage lights begin to blink for everyone to take their seats.

The ex-girlfriend gazes ferociously into the face of the Future Candidate.

There may be some longing here.

There may be loathing.

The ex-girlfriend leads the next move.

It is professional, an expert flick of her leg over his calf.

A swift trabada.

Rapturously in sync now,

the Future Candidate dips the ex-girlfriend again, lower.

As the music ends,

he brings his lips to her throat.

During the first scene of his brother's play, all Victor could think about were the bones in Lena's wrist, the tension of them under his grip.

He was certain no one had seen him grab hold of her that hard. With everyone pushed up against each other in the lobby, who could've seen?

Certainly not Cristina. He'd cut between them, and grabbing a woman's wrist for a second couldn't implicate a man. It was the sort of transgression that, if mentioned as proof of anything, would sound exaggerated, oversensitive. All he'd done was startle Lena enough to prevent her from saying Maria's name again, to make Lena gasp instead, and hadn't she asked for it, marching so righteously across the lobby with that dilettante bitterness of hers, with her deceptively delicate-looking mouth?

It was possible Freddy had seen. But what his brother saw didn't matter. Freddy would understand why he'd lost control for a second. Seeing Lena after so long—all the Molotovs he'd made and thrown with her, the adrenaline-fueled twenty-year-old sex they'd had after setting two police cars aflame and fleeing up that interminable stairwell into the hills. Sitting in the dark theater, Victor pressed his tongue against the roof of his mouth, recalling how triumphantly he'd submerged his very same tongue between Lena's legs that night, had pressed his whole mouth and teeth into her until she opened her thighs, wider.

It wasn't until the second scene of Freddy's play that he brought his mind to bear on what was happening in front of him, on the stage. The play was set in a gay bar but the leading actor wasn't another version of Freddy this time. The lead was a closeted married man, a father who loathed himself for being unable to resist the lure of the bar and the men inside it. A father whose sister had been killed in the roundups, but who otherwise was more or less their father, which was ludicrous. It was libelous.

It was outright lunacy.

Victor watched in horror as the father figure on the stage danced alone with a purple feather boa.

Along the back of Victor's neck he felt a scalding, spreading heat.

His brother had crossed the line this time. Their father hadn't broken into rages all the time because he wanted to stick it into a man. He'd been in a rage because his brother hadn't been released, and they didn't have the money or contacts to find out what had been done to him. Their father had brooded in the same bars all the other bitter men in their neighborhood brooded in, their bodies tense and agitated from having to constantly listen for police cars and watch over their shoulders, knowing they might be picked up for anything at all, and the same could happen to their sons. Their father hadn't snuck off to some bar to dance with transvestites.

Victor swore under his breath and turned his head. Two seats away, Freddy was staring at his blasphemous creation with a pleased little smile. Freddy, who hadn't even had the balls to warn him beforehand, although he had told Victor about the interview in the paper. When Freddy asked on the phone if he'd read it, Victor had lied and said congratulations. What was he going to do, admit he'd felt such revulsion at the photo of his brother in that ridiculous velvet scarf that he couldn't get through even the first paragraph of the interview? And there was no pressuring Freddy to change anything now. All he could do was go on sitting there in the dark theater, expressionless in his seat, as if he were some cutout of a man fashioned from cardboard.

Beside him, his fiancée pulled her cell phone out of her purse again to check the time. But somewhere behind him, Lena was undoubtedly grasping it all, relishing how he must be loathing every second of this scene. But he didn't have to give Lena that power. No one else had ever taken her seriously. She had gone nowhere. She was nothing.

From the meager contents of Lena's fridge, all Oscar could think to make was an omelet. Besides eggs and cheese, the fridge didn't contain much beyond a bowl of shriveled-up grapes and a few condiments. He hadn't expected Lena to accept his offer to come inside and throw together some food for them. But when he asked if she was hungry and wanted him to make something, she'd replied with an emphatic yes and held open the door.

He'd hoped to conjure up something more impressive but there had been so little to work with and the effort to understand the dialogue in the play had fatigued his brain. It had taken him two scenes to realize the play was about a closeted gay father during the Cato regime. He hadn't expected the staging to be so subtle either, with the actors abruptly swaying and tilting their heads midline, as if being pulled into a dance with an invisible partner. Every minute of it had been exquisite, even the title—*Where He Danced While We Lay Dreaming*.

Even the intermission had been unlike anything he'd ever experienced in a theater. A couple had announced their engagement, and everyone had raised their plastic cups of wine and cheered. Lena hadn't joined the cheering, though he was fairly certain it was the same couple she had approached before the show. Still, Oscar hadn't felt certain enough of this to ask. He felt ashamed of how similar the men on the island still looked to him. Afraid to risk revealing this inadequacy to Lena, he hadn't inquired if it was the same man she'd approached earlier. Despite his deliberate effort to tell them apart, he still kept confusing the two brothers who worked at his hostel, who had the same buzzed hair and compact build.

And now, as he cracked the eggs and glanced outside her kitchen window, he saw a man of similar height and build leaning against a car, smoking, and staring back at him with an eerie steadiness. Is that guy your neighbor? he asked.

What guy? Lena drew up next to him, her arm knocking the bowl of eggs, causing the contents to splash over her shirt and drip in rivulets onto the floor. Ugh, I'm sorry, she said as Oscar bent to scoop the yolks off the edge of the counter as best he could, insisting it was his fault for leaving the bowl there.

But Lena's focus was solely on the man outside. Where is he? Where did you see him standing? she asked.

Oscar stood up with the yolky rag to show her but the man was no longer at the curb. He craned his neck to look up and down the street but couldn't see the man anywhere.

Lena insisted she needed to know what the man looked like in detail, and he apologized. Between the dark and the distance all he could think to describe for her was the two brothers who managed his hostel.

He hoped it wouldn't matter. The man had gone.

The man had gone, Lena reassured herself.

He'd gone because he was meaningless—just some drunk lingering for a moment on his way up from the bars at the bottom of the hill. But what if he wasn't? She'd seen the fury on Victor's face when he crushed her wrist, the tendons bulging in his neck when she said the name Maria.

But he couldn't have abandoned his fiancée so soon after the play, and there must have been some kind of feud between him and Freddy for portraying a character obviously meant to evoke their father. Lena had found the play moving and tender, and clearly intended as no more than conjecture, an attempt to understand why their father had been either absent or explosive. But she knew Victor wouldn't be able to see it on those terms. When Freddy spoke about his lovers, Victor always tensed and got up from the table. She could only imagine Victor's reaction to seeing a version of his father dance with another man on a stage.

With all of that happening, she decided, Victor couldn't possibly have extracted himself to come lurk for a few threatening minutes outside her house. But maybe, as a senator, he could have come up with an excuse to send some menacing emissary to do it for him. She'd never seen any drunks pause at night in front of her house and stare in her kitchen window, but perhaps they had and she hadn't noticed, as she had failed to notice the large stain on the jean jacket she'd left lying on her bed. While Oscar cracked a new batch of eggs in the kitchen, she'd retreated to her room to change shirts.

But for now, she just stood at the end of the bed, startled to see such a large stain on her jacket. It extended across the entire back and down one of its sleeves. Before Freddy's show, she'd pulled the jacket out of the closet but had decided to wear her warmer wool coat instead. Even distracted and nervous, she was certain that she would have noticed a stain that large when she dropped the jacket on her bed. The stain looked dark enough to be wine, though she couldn't recall any spilled wine the last time she wore the jacket. When she entered the room, she'd only flicked on the small light by her dresser and wondered if maybe it was just a strangely shaped shadow. But of what?

She felt too disturbed to move toward the closet to flick on the other lamp by the window. The stain looked definitively reddish to her now, the muddy color of a period stain, and copious, saturating the cotton of her jacket as if someone had slowly died in it.

She felt a coldness shudder up through her body. Sucking in her breath, she wondered if she was having a breakdown. Wasn't this one of the ways women unraveled? They failed to marry at the expected age, they got lonelier, stuck on some ex-lover's success while they remained trapped in one demoralizing position after another, their thoughts growing increasingly erratic and unhinged.

She wondered if she should ask Oscar to leave or to stay. Whether the stain was connected to Maria or not, a man had just been lurking outside her house. Oscar had seen him. And there would be other nights to come when she'd be alone here. Her murder would be written off as the sort of random crime that happened to rich girls who became heedless bohemians instead of sticking to their own, who thought they could live on some dark street in the most dilapidated part of the port and get away with it. A consequence of her own poor judgment. Her arrogance.

She crawled onto the bed and lowered her face to smell the stain. At the thought of the man outside, of Victor seizing her wrist in the lobby, she could not bring herself to lift the jacket, to find out what might pass onto her hands if she held it. The only smells she could detect on the fabric were the ones on all her clothes: the powdery scent of her deodorant, marijuana from Olga's, and something else slightly musty and female—her body itself, perhaps, the faint odor of a woman trying to live with a degree of resignation that was at odds with her nature.

Your omelet, Oscar called from the kitchen, is now flipped and ready!

It was not quite dawn when Victor rose from Cristina's bed. Outside her magnificent windows, the horizon was empty of ships, the only movement the searching dots of gulls circling over the water. He didn't realize Cristina had risen as well until her hands came around his bare waist and she sank her fingers into his pubic hair. I hope it's me you're standing here thinking about, she said.

I'm thinking about the play, Victor said. I can't go after my own brother for defamation, and that kind of attention would only backfire.

He waited for Cristina to commiserate or at least withdraw her hands and leave him to his thoughts. But he was beginning to learn she had no reverence for introspection. She never read, not even magazines, and instead of leaving him alone she began to stroke him.

She had been right, though, that her body was not the one he'd woken up thinking about. And Freddy hadn't really been the reason he'd bolted from the bed. He'd gone to the windows to stop repeatedly seizing Lena's wrist in his mind, convincing himself the way she sucked in her breath hadn't been alarm—or not only alarm. It had been arousal, too. He hadn't lost control. He'd been responding to her face. She'd wanted him to grab hold of her somehow. She'd marched over looking for it.

He brushed his hand over Cristina's so she would continue her maneuvers, go about them even faster. Just as he'd relaxed enough to close his eyes, Cristina started nattering in a nervous, nasal way about a pig farm, of all things, in the interior. Some farmer who was a friend of her father's who'd run into some bad luck with an inspector acting like a fascist. Her father was hoping Victor wouldn't mind making a call to the cousin of his who worked in the Agricultural Department.

I didn't want to bring it up last night at the play, Cristina said, continuing with her rubbing, but I think it's my father's way of reaching out, you know, between men. You don't mind calling, do you?

Transaction Log for Olga's
SEEK THE SUBLIME OR DIE

September 9th

Yet another Saturday begun, S, with a joint in bed.

And not a single book sale to report yet for the morning.

And nothing sublime about doing the side business, though it keeps the lights on, which have never been cheap on this beleaguered island your family has probably all left by now. I think of them, S, the regrets that must accompany your brother, and your quiet mother if she's still around, somewhere.

Reluctant Nonliterary Income
Buyers: two students gushing about Victor taking the free tuition bill to the Senate as if he were the second coming of Che Guevara.

I'll never say it to Lena, but if Victor did push that girl, he's going to get away with it. The road was empty. There were no witnesses. Maybe Che Guevara disposed of some inconvenient girl like a soda can as well. Maybe he disposed of several.

Who wants to hear it? People are too desperate for a hero.

If you were alive, S, if you were here now, sitting on the couch in Conspiracy, you would likely identify this thought as a sign of my descent into an ever more self-defeating cynicism, and you would be correct.

I go on selling pot to students who smoke far too much of it. But if I didn't, someone else would, and at least they're coming into a bookstore for their joints, right? At least a bookstore exists on this hill and they have to pass a table of paperbacks to get their weed. Oh, the compromises and justifications one comes to make by late middle age, S, they are humiliating.

9:26, The Question
How did Joan of Arc do it, S? How did she stay true to the voices in her head as they led her into the fire?

From *The Weekender* Profile

The Weekender: Many students and parents find the campus takeovers happening all over the island too disruptive. If students care so much about their education, why don't they find some other way to protest, some strategy that doesn't postpone half a semester's worth of learning?

Senator Victor MG: Because protests have to be disruptive. If this protest weren't disruptive, you wouldn't be interviewing me about the outrageous debt even middle-class families have to take on to educate their children. And what other nonviolent form of dissent is there?

We have a long history of importing the worst aspects of the foreign government that so ruinously intervened in this one—their tolerance for police brutality as long as it's reserved for the poor, their dismantling of unions. We don't need their exclusive vacation resort approach toward higher education any more than we need their fast-food chains or their disgusting Galaxy bars replacing our own chocolate.

The Weekender: You don't eat Galaxy bars?

Senator Victor MG: Absolutely not. My brother let himself get addicted to them but I've never eaten one. And I never will.

SCENES FROM *THE PRUNING OF A FUTURE PRESIDENTIAL CANDIDATE*
(WORK IN PROGRESS OF FMG)

Late childhood in the Cato years

SET

Stage is bare except for a large cardboard Galaxy chocolate bar.

The chocolate bar should hang from ropes that allow it to swing easily.

It should be taller and larger than the child actors.

Two brothers, ages eight and five, emerge from opposite sides of the stage.

They stop on either side of the Galaxy bar.

YOUNGER BROTHER

I want to know what it tastes like.

OLDER BROTHER

We're not opening it.

YOUNGER BROTHER

But Dad's cousin brought it all this way for us.

OLDER BROTHER

But you heard what he told her. Our uncle died because
people here don't care about anything but getting TV sets
from the fucking north.

YOUNGER BROTHER

What's the fucking north?

OLDER BROTHER

You know what it is. Where all the blond people in the
movies live. Dad says they—

*With animal ferocity, the younger brother bites into the
Galaxy bar.*

The older brother yanks it from him.

The younger one pulls it back.

The Galaxy bar swings wildly between them.

Abruptly, the older brother changes his strategy.

He shoves the chocolate toward his brother instead of away.

*The surprise knocks the younger boy down and he begins
to cry.*

OLDER BROTHER

Stop it, don't act like a baby.

If you cry every time you want to know

what some plastic-wrapped candy tastes like,

you'll cry the rest of your life.

You have to control yourself.

Pick a spot on the wall

and stare at it like a senator.

Like this.

The older brother turns, fixes his gaze on the audience.

He remains this way,

grim-faced as a military statue.

The younger brother, still on his knees,

bites into the chocolate.

He releases a groan of pleasure.

The lights dim.

The Galaxy bar collapses on top of him.

Beneath it, he goes on munching.

His groans of pleasure blast from the speakers.

The groans turn into the contented purr of cats,

then the happy nicker of horses,

while the stage goes dark.

Traditional Sunday lunch on the island was an extended affair. When Lena arrived, just getting through all her family's kisses and questions took an hour. With each relative came another round of Haven't you tired of living above that filthy port yet? Don't you want to live somewhere cleaner and safer, and what about a boyfriend, eh? We're all waiting.

She no longer braced for questions about her role in the marches. No one in the family bothered to try to persuade her anymore with their justifications for the regime. When she'd taught in the island's municipal schools, her aunts had occasionally asked if the children in them were as out of control as they imagined. Lena had tried to explain that the problem with the municipal system was the number of children packed into the classrooms, not the children themselves, but she knew it didn't matter. Her aunts drew the unflattering conclusions about the island's children that they wanted to draw anyway.

Lena had wanted to stick it out teaching in the municipal system just to defy her family. But the truth was, keeping children in their chairs and focused had not been the right fit for her. She'd gotten impatient and missed hearing the ideas of adults, of discussing education in the philosophical way she had in college. Now that she had a position more acceptable to her family, her aunts and sisters-in-law were single-mindedly focused on her potential for procreation. Every week they would descend upon her like vultures to peck at her with estimates of how many years she had left to bear a child.

Yet the subtext of these warnings, Lena suspected, was not really their desire for her to be a mother. It was their collective hope that in motherhood she might become one of them again, which made

Lena only more leery of marrying, of falling into any pattern her mother and aunts might perceive as proof that she would eventually rejoin their ranks.

Well before the unavoidable round of Sunday Warnings, however, came the locked gate in the wall that rimmed her family's home. Then came the driveway with her family's squadron of Land Rovers— her father's and grandfather's, and those of her twin brothers, who were ten years older and now worked at Sunny Juice as well. Her uncle was the only liberal in the family and the only man in the family who didn't drive a Land Rover. He was also the only one who had never walled in his home even though he'd been robbed several times, including once when he'd hidden himself in the closet in the maid's room off the kitchen, which the thieves didn't bother to enter.

As Lena passed her uncle's compact two-door tucked like a toy behind the Land Rovers, she thought of her small first-floor home, how she'd have nowhere in it to hide if whoever Oscar had seen lurking outside came back and tried to break in. That morning when she woke up, she had checked her jacket and found no stain on it, which only increased her fear that her perceptions were becoming unreliable. How had she let herself become such a nervous wreck last night, too paralyzed to even turn on her own lamp?

Opening the second gate to her family's garden, she knew she had to get a hold of herself.

She was well past the roses now and fully visible to her family. One of her nephews on the swing set had already spotted her and jumped off the slide. He ran over and held up his arms for her to pick him up and she did, grateful for the simple, physical pleasure of squeezing such a small being, of pressing his little warm face against her own.

My queen! her mother called, rushing up next.

My rebel! her beloved uncle said as he approached, his deep, resonant voice overtaking her mother's, and Lena wrapped her arms around her small, bald uncle with relief.

I assume you've seen this, he said, tapping her with the weekend magazine. There's an interview with your senator from the port talking up his free tuition plan. He's really stirring up the students again, isn't he? Though he sounds like a rather rigid creature, to go after his own brother in an interview for eating a chocolate bar that's been in every gas station in the country for years. But I bet you adore this guy, right? Your students must be crazy about him.

Lena took the magazine from her uncle before he could tap her shoulder with it again.

Victor hunched closer to the microphone to shout over the jingle of the ice cream truck passing along the other end of the park. He hated speaking on Sunday afternoons, although he'd been the one who'd told the students they needed to organize rallies on the weekends, when more working people would be able to stop and listen. He had no one but himself to blame for being stuck again, both days this weekend, behind a microphone.

Social progress, he shouted into it, never happens without a battle! No government has ever granted greater access to education without people gathering like we are doing right now, in the street on a Sunday, and demanding it. No seat in any university on this planet was given to a poor kid whose family couldn't pay for it without an all-out revolt. All of you out here giving your Sunday afternoon to fight for everyone's access to an education, you're the reason every newspaper and every member of Congress is paying attention. And you're the reason it will happen!

Victor waited a beat for the cheers and shouts to die down. The fish chowder he'd had with Cristina and her family for lunch had been too rich and heavy. He wished he were on his couch at home, or could at least loosen his belt. Gripping the podium more tightly, he stiffened his face, waiting for the distended feeling in his stomach to subside.

Because it will happen, he repeated, and I will be here fighting with you until it does! He shouted louder, forcing the passion in his voice as if it were a horse beneath him and if he just kicked at it hard enough he could get it to gallop. By the end of his remarks, his pulse was racing, the urgency overtaking him. When a pretty student turned off the mike and offered him a new bottle of water, he gulped it standing up.

God, I could listen to you speak all day, she gushed, flicking her hair behind her shoulder. It's like listening to a preacher. You have that kind of resolute belief. It really moves people.

Victor smiled as he set the empty water bottle down on the podium. He liked that choice of word, resolute, and she really was quite attractive, fawn-like, with her large, thick-lashed brown eyes and slender arms. Keen intelligence in a delicate face like that had such an alluring radiance, and the widow's peak at her hairline was striking, too.

Victor asked what she was studying and watched how the girl's eyes widened in response to his interest, how judiciously she articulated her answers in pursuit of his approval. It was like a perfume, to be on the receiving end of that kind of eagerness, of a young woman's gratitude for his willingness to hear her out. No, it was stronger than a fragrance—inhaling the yearning in a girl for him to recognize her intelligence, to reiterate even one thing she said that had impressed him. Other people were lining up behind her but Victor ignored them.

Already in your last term in political science, he said, how excellent. I hope you'll consider something with the government when you graduate. I mean that. We really need more smart young women in office—in absolutely every position.

When the girl sucked in her breath, Victor suggested she contact his office the following spring about working on his reelection campaign. We'll just be getting started. He met her eyes and watched her nervously flick her hair again, felt his body willing itself closer. But then a diesel bus roared to a stop along the edge of the park just behind them. At the sound of its hissing brakes, he stepped away.

Oscar wandered twice around the fish market, wishing he knew what to do with himself and his dwindling inheritance. He stopped at one display after another, studied the fish scales glistening behind the glass like sequins. He wished he knew if Lena even liked fish, or what her phone number was. He didn't even know her last name. After their omelets Friday night, Lena had led him to the front door and said good night with no more than a perfunctory kiss on the cheek. For all he knew, she would be appalled that he was returning this soon and uninvited, annoyed that he'd wrongly assumed he could just show up again with an offering of fish and zucchini.

But was there not—and there was—also a slim chance she might welcome the sight of him and his offer to show what kind of dinner he could assemble with a proper set of ingredients? She'd told him his omelet was the best she'd ever eaten. Maybe this time he'd even get to stay the night.

At the thought, he bought the thickest, whitest piece of fish in the display, labeled under a local name he didn't recognize. Outside the market, he hailed a taxi.

A cold, damp darkness was descending over the hills around the port by the time he arrived at Lena's front door. A light was on in her kitchen but no one answered. She'd told him on Friday that she saw her family most Sundays but got tired of them by late afternoon and headed home.

He knocked again, certain he had the right place. None of the other houses on her street had a purple door, and through the window he recognized the green squiggles painted on the backs of her kitchen chairs. The chilly evening wind off the ocean pressed against him and he shivered, squinting harder through the window. He'd made over a dozen cheddar scones, and it had been such a lonely Sunday, though all his Sundays in the hostel were lonely, watching families laughing together on their way into the seafood restaurant across the road.

After a few more minutes of squinting and self-pity, a giant Land Rover pulled up, white and gleaming as a chariot. The passenger door opened and Lena emerged with her lovely heart-shaped face. She pointed at him and made a remark to whoever was inside the car. When she reached the porch, she kissed him on the mouth. Can you wave at my brother? she asked. He was alarmed that you were sitting out here. I had to tell him we've been dating for a while or he wouldn't leave.

No problem at all. Oscar jauntily placed his arm around her shoulders and waved at the man in the Land Rover. He'd assumed from Lena's modest first-floor rental that her family was working class. He hoped her brother wasn't involved in some kind of shady business, or a drug cartel. Once again, fearful of saying something potentially ignorant or offensive, he didn't ask about her brother's line of work or even his name. Inside, he went right to slicing the zucchini.

Lena put on a soulful melancholy song and he tried to make out what the chorus was about. The song was in the language spoken on the island but the singer seemed to have a different accent. He asked Lena where the song was from and she named a country on the mainland, where the language was also spoken. She told him it was a protest song about the long presence of his army there.

I've never thought of it that way, as my army. Technically, I guess that's true. Oscar slid the zucchini into the pan and told her he knew the regime there had been particularly bad but couldn't remember the name of the head of it or why his government had gotten so involved.

I never did well on history exams, he confessed, spreading the slivers of zucchini out more evenly across the pan. I always wanted to remember the dates and names, but they just didn't stick. He shrugged. I guess I'm basically just a pastry and poetry man.

He saw Lena press her lips together with disdain at this confession and Oscar lowered his head, regretting his honesty. But once Lena tried his cheddar scones, the pinched judgmental expression on her face went away, and after she finished the fish, she placed her hand over his and sighed with pleasure.

Beneath the table, he ventured a brush of her knee. While he scrubbed the dishes, he gave a few furtive checks for anybody outside the window but saw no one. Lena didn't bring up the man he'd seen outside, and Oscar didn't either. When she drifted from the kitchen to the living room, he followed, his hope rising like dough inside him.

Transaction Log for Olga's
SEEK THE SUBLIME OR DIE

September 10th

All cheap tea and unease today, S.

Still no news from Lena. She hasn't called or come by since she came in here full of trust and I shut her down. I left two messages on her machine. I hope she's just disgusted with me and the reason she hasn't answered isn't Victor. If there is an art to emotional isolation, S, I have mastered it spectacularly.

On the other hand, Oscar the Baker has not loped in here all weekend either.

Out of guilt, I loaned a copy of your favorite translation of *Requiem* to a girl who buys far too much weed.

Official Sales Report for the Tenth of September
No income whatsoever.

Unofficial Report
A girl with blue hair and a large mole on her cheek may read a line or two today of the poet you called the Goddess Akhmatova. I told her if she learns a stanza of *Requiem* by heart and comes back able to recite it, the book is hers to keep. But I shouldn't have bothered calling it a loan in the first place. She probably won't come back

at all. Most likely she sensed my desperation and was relieved to get out of here and away from me.

4:49, Sunday Panic

I'm starting to crack along every seam, S, like the derelict swimming pool of some abandoned ranch in the interior. Maybe everyone who comes into the Sublime and steps close enough now can see it—my loneliness seeping out all over the place.

Victor woke from a nap in his office to the thought of pigs. Of their little twisted-up tails. Their vile squeals. The sickening stink of them. He did not want to ruin his Monday afternoon coercing his cousin to grant a permit for a thousand more pigs to some man neither of them knew anything about. He knew his cousin would say that many pigs would mean that many more kilos of shit, which had to be dumped somewhere, and which was surely the reason this phone call was necessary. What political favors were not ultimately about pig shit and how to get rid of it?

But it was too late to reconsider. Their engagement news had run in *The Islander* this morning with a quote from his soon-to-be father-in-law about how much he admired Victor's history of activism and his bold ideas for how to provide a free college education for any student who qualified. His father-in-law had set up a lunch for him next week with a journalist who covered the island for the London *Times*. He insisted Victor needed to start getting his name in papers beyond the island. Their tacit exchange of favors was already under way. In every email he received now, a mention of his father-in-law surfaced within the first few lines. The wedding date hadn't even been determined yet and Victor already felt like a political pet, expected to roll over on request, to repeatedly perform his gratitude for the shelter he'd been given.

On the other hand, when he'd arrived at Cristina's, she'd had a tremendous lobster waiting for him. She'd also answered the door in a lace robe and nothing on underneath it. There were certainly worse ways for a man to end a workday.

Victor pushed back in his chair and lifted his feet up onto the desk. Once he had them comfortably crossed, he clicked down to his cousin's number on his cell phone. Hadn't his mother told him a few months ago that his cousin was engaged? She loved to berate him with the news of other people's engagements.

Congratulations, Victor said when his cousin answered, I heard you're heading down the aisle soon.

His cousin laughed and said he'd just read the same in the paper about Victor, and to such an influential family.

You're really moving up in the world, his cousin said. I'm proud of you.

Victor brought his feet to the ground, his mind filling with the sickening squeals of pigs—their little dirty behinds releasing pile after vile pile of shit—and he did not want to ask the question.

But he did.

While Oscar slept on blondly beside her, their second morning together in bed, Lena thought about her students gathering again today with their signs, the questions they were going to ask about her absence during the strike. She'd have to invent a convincing health problem, something severe but easily resolved—an abscessed molar, maybe, that had caused a high fever and required urgent oral surgery. Whatever she said, her credibility on campus would be diminished regardless.

In May, when the students first started organizing, she'd invited them over to help with flyers and strategies. She'd ordered them pizzas and planned to offer as much of her time and guidance as they asked of her. But then Victor started showing up at the protests, promising to take their demands to the Senate. The more involved he became, the more she'd withdrawn and holed up at the Sublime. With Victor's presence, the news cameras arrived and Olga assured her that other professors would come forward to help and have their pictures taken—and they had. The head of her department, who'd done nothing until then, had immediately strutted up to the reporters to announce his commitment to the strike and declare Victor the most laudable candidate for president in years.

Following it all online, Lena had felt muted, the volume of her existence on zero except for her hours with Olga. Impersonating the head of her department and making each other laugh as they stacked books and smoked together had felt alchemical, the only way to spin her anger into something bearable—or at least until the evening, when she was alone again in front of her computer, scrolling through the latest commanding poses of Victor in the news.

But there would be no way to convey any of this to her students. No matter what health crisis she invented when the strike ended, she'd still be the professor who lectured about social action who hadn't been there.

Under the sheets, she clenched her toes and rolled onto her side to distract herself with Oscar, how white-blond his hair was even in his armpit. She had never slept with such a pale man. How had she let an entire Monday go by doing nothing but baking and having sex with this freckled man whose country had bankrolled Cato?

When her cell phone rang in the living room, she didn't move to answer it. She just went on staring at the startling lunar whiteness of Oscar's skin above the T-shirt line on his arm. She had not expected the wave of affection that came over her when Oscar washed the whole sink full of dishes without demanding any applause. He had just done it, scrubbed one pan after another and with such unassuming expertise.

When they'd wandered naked into the kitchen for some water and he suggested they bake something, she had been surprised how readily a yes escaped her. Whatever song she put on, Oscar had hummed along to her choices, and it occurred to her he had no urgency to resume his life at the hostel, would likely stay on at her place if she asked him, keeping her company until the strike ended and she returned to class. If she gave him the right encouragement, he'd probably stay on even longer. Then she scolded herself for indulging in such a thought. She didn't belong with some oblivious, uninformed northerner.

Although what a reprieve it had been to have sex with someone who didn't make even a single subtle reference to her family, to feel no pressure to denounce them for once, to dismiss her Sundays as no more than obligation. She had been so grateful when Oscar waved at her brother without a single snide remark about his Land Rover.

Even after they went inside, Oscar hadn't inquired what her brother did to afford such an extravagant car rarely seen in the hills

above the port. To kiss a man who understood none of the conno-
tations of her country had been like a vacation from herself. She had
felt relieved from her own gravity, from the continual pressure of
having to decide how much self-recrimination any given conversation
required.

Yanking the sheet up to her face, she curled closer to Oscar's long,
pale arm. Olga had to be right about the zigzag sweater, about
her failing to notice the cashier tucking it back into her tote bag. The
bra, too, could have ended up in her drawer from some mix-up while
doing laundry at her parents' house last summer. Either of her sisters-
in-law could be the owner of a lacy white push-up bra like that.

Yes, Lena decided, rolling onto her back again, there were explanations for all of it. And if Maria wanted to haunt someone with the
truth, why would she pick someone with such an abhorrent family
history that would cancel out anything Lena might try to reveal?

Or was it the shock last night of Victor's grip again on her wrist
that had rendered her suddenly this passive and limp? She had not
even asked Oscar to put on a condom.

Clenching her jaw, Lena launched herself out of bed and pulled
some leggings from the heap of clothes on her desk chair.

The phone rang again. To avoid waking Oscar, she answered,
assuming it must be her mother, eager for more details about the
northerner her brother had seen on the porch.

It's too early, Mother, she said.

It's me, her brother said. Is your boyfriend watching the attack?
Where's he from there? It's crazy.

What attack? Lena shuffled into the living room in her slippers
to look for the remote. Her TV had belonged to her parents. They'd
replaced it with a larger one and she mostly used it for watching
movies. It took a minute to find a working channel with the news,
and even then it was a fuzzy feed of an immense, distant building,
the upper half of it in flames. Beside it, another structure was en-
gulfed in smoke.

The image switched to a street full of screaming, fleeing people, zooming in on a man half carrying a woman in ripped stockings to the curb. Lena turned up the volume and waited to hear the creak of her bed planks on the other side of the wall. But she heard no sound from the next room as she went on watching the smoke billow and darken above the buildings.

Oscar, she called and shook her head, surprised that he could sleep on this soundly in the home of someone he barely knew. She called again a little louder and heard a yawn—her long, freckled guest finally stirring in her sheets.

Oscar sucked in his breath and leaned forward. How was this possible? This sort of incomprehensible thing didn't happen in his country. Lena called to him from the kitchen about coffee but he didn't answer. His mouth had begun to feel as numb as his legs from kneeling too long in front of the TV. But it felt wrong to extract himself from the position to be more comfortable. He knew the exact corner the newscaster was standing on, had stood at the top of the tower that had just collapsed. One summer, before dropping out of college, he'd done a culinary program just one street down from where a fleet of grim-faced emergency workers were strapping a motionless, bloodied man in a dark suit onto a gurney.

He shivered and leaned closer. He'd only pulled on his boxers before rushing out to watch the TV, and Lena's living room was as poorly insulated and drafty as her bedroom.

A different newscaster came on. In a thin, bewildered voice, she reported that the second tower was expected to collapse as well, and a moment later, smoke plumed from it as if from the mouth of a volcano. Oscar let out an anguished cry.

Here. Lena arrived with his mug of coffee in one hand, one of his cheddar scones in the other. He heard her crunch into the scone and a current of disgust jolted through him. How can you eat with this happening? he asked.

Are you serious? I've been standing here watching since before you woke up. Just take your mug, she said, it's heavy.

Lena thrust the coffee at him. All her mugs were large, heavy ceramic things, and her fingers looked too thin and delicate for such a determined gesture. In bed he had found her surprisingly meek—even passive—and he felt disoriented now, kneeling beneath her on the thin wool rug in his paisley boxers, the mug still hovering between them, the blare of sirens taking over the living room.

A river of people was now pouring from the corner where he'd turned to reach the culinary school. It's incomprehensible, he murmured.

Is it, though? Lena slammed his coffee down on top of the TV and Oscar glanced up at her, disturbed to find his gaze drawn even now to her breasts, loose under the worn cotton of her pajama shirt.

What are you doing? She crossed her arms. You can stare at my chest while your country's being attacked, but I can't eat a bite of breakfast?

Lena, don't be ridiculous, he said. I wasn't staring that way.

Oh come on, Mr. Poetry and Pastry Man. You were. I can't eat because your city is the one on fire for once but you can stare at my chest because you're the northerner and you get to set the rules for everyone. That's how it's always gone, right? Just admit it, she said, moving in front of the TV, blocking his view.

Please, I'm sorry, Lena. Just let me see what's happening. Still on his knees, he tilted his head to see around her.

I'll move when you admit it, she said. If those people were dying anywhere but in your country, would you have cared if I went on eating your scone? I bet you wouldn't.

On the TV screen, an older blond man bleeding through his ripped oxford shirt looked so eerily like his father that Oscar shot up from the floor. He heard Lena repeat her question, her voice furious now, but he rushed past her toward the open door of her bedroom. Lena followed close behind him, still clutching her mug, demanding to know if his parents stopped drinking their coffee for even a second when his government supplied the trucks to round up Olga and thousands of others. To shoot them down on the street.

I know what my government did here, Lena. He yanked his pants on, his legs still tingling. I know I can only guess how horrific it was, but that was in part why I wanted to come here, to understand.

Oh, is that so? Lena clenched her face and stepped closer. And is this part of your understanding, screwing women who are supposed to feel grateful and lucky when you show up with dinner for them? Well, guess what? I don't need your fucking scone! Lena hurled it to the floor.

Oscar lowered his head, too winded to respond or do up the buttons on his pants. He wanted to tell her she was the only person he'd been with in over a year, nearly two. But he could barely maintain enough composure to reach for his sneakers. He had felt radiant falling asleep beside her. Well after midnight, they'd gotten hungry and made crêpes in their underwear, had sung along together to a rock song from his country that everyone in the hemisphere knew. By the last chorus, they were half dancing through the flour on the floor, and he'd felt a joy so delicate it felt invented, some new kind of twenty-first-century joy, so unexpected it was breathtaking, causing the very air in the kitchen to shimmer.

Leaving Lena's bedroom now, he didn't stop to tie the laces of his sneakers. He just fumbled toward the hall, open-shoed, dumbstruck, cupping his hands over his ears as he had as a child during fire drills. But he heard Lena behind him anyhow, yelling that his kind of willful imperialist ignorance was the worst, the most unforgivable.

In the living room, he heard people on the TV crying and shouting. As he passed the screen, he felt as if he were fleeing with them, wailing with them even if he was in another hemisphere, even if all that awaited him at the end of Lena's narrow hall was the steep, winding curve of her road. For a moment, in her drafty room last night, he had imagined what it would be like to move in, to wake over and over next to Lena, to come to know her books stacked in the corners, to belong to her.

When her door slammed behind him, he felt incapable of starting up the hill. At the curb, he came to a stop, unable to do anything

but fixate on a crushed soda can in the closest pothole, all the terrified people in the city he loved, with their bloody arms and ash-
streaked faces, still running in every direction through his mind.

From down the hill came the moan of an engine. A moment later,
a rusted blue Volkswagen Beetle labored around the curve. The
woman coaxing her ancient vehicle up the hill was young and hum-
ming along with the radio as if it were any day at all in human
history. As she passed him, she flicked a tissue out the window.

Olga was rolling her morning joint and listening to the radio report on humanity's latest destruction of itself when her door jangled. Wild-eyed, wet-haired, Lena entered the bookstore. Olga never rose to greet anyone who entered but she pushed herself up now from the sunken seat of her velvet chair. The abruptness of the rise left her dizzy. She motioned for her friend to come around the register, and Lena stepped past the edge of it without a word.

Olga held out her arms and for the first time in what felt like centuries she pulled someone into her embrace tightly enough to feel Lena's body press against her own. She felt Lena's breath against her ear. She kissed the top of her friend's head and it felt maternal, sensual—that fragile, erotic overlap that can happen in an embrace between two people who have gradually become essential to one another but have yet to speak of it, and who will likely never speak of all the shoved-down wadded-up things they have come to silently glimpse inside each other.

She pressed her lips against her friend's wet hair and knew this would likely be the last time she held someone this way. She had not realized she had come to feel protective enough of Lena to include her among the few people for whom she would place herself in the line of fire. For whom she would extract her knife if things came to that. At all times, since returning to the island, she had maintained a formidable knife under her armchair in the likelihood that some-day things would come to that.

SCENES FROM *THE PRUNING* *OF A FUTURE PRESIDENTIAL CANDIDATE*
(WORK IN PROGRESS BY FMG)

In the last months of the Cato years.

SET

A picnic table.

A cardboard moon hangs from a string to indicate the time is evening.

If possible, dangle a few aluminum foil stars to accompany the moon.

A college-age girl sits at the table next to her boyfriend.

They are facing the audience.

On the other side, his back to the public,

sits the boyfriend's younger, chubby brother.

They are playing dominoes.

Among the domino chips, there could be a few bottles of beer.

GIRL

Hey, stop looking at my dominoes!

FUTURE CANDIDATE

I'm not looking. I don't need to. I'm going to win anyway.

GIRL

You don't know that.

FUTURE CANDIDATE

I do know, I always beat you both.

Neither of you is ruthless enough.

LITTLE BROTHER

I am!

I'm ruthless enough.

GIRL

Do you see how you're corrupting his soul?

FUTURE CANDIDATE

His soul is corrupted already.

Everybody who grew up under Cato has soul damage.

GIRL

But being damaged doesn't mean you have an excuse for
ruthlessness.

LITTLE BROTHER

I just want to win for once!

The future candidate laughs.

He pats his little brother on the head as if he were a small, harmless dog.

The little brother barks.

The girlfriend lets out a melancholy howl.

The future candidate does not acknowledge the sounds they are making.

Head bent over the table, he rearranges his dominoes.

FUTURE CANDIDATE

Okay, pets, take some notes.

Check out that double six.

See, I knew neither of you had any sixes left.

Only me.

To win, you have to hide what you have more of than anyone else.

Whether you like it or not, that's how the ruthless win.

Four years later
in the most dominant city
of the most dominant country

Four years after the death of Maria P. was declared an accident, Lena was living abroad, pushing her son on the swings, when she heard someone speaking her language with a familiar cadence. She had come for a doctorate at one of the most renowned universities in the hemisphere and rarely ran into anyone from the island whom she didn't already know.

But she didn't recognize this woman with dark hair in a loose braid on the next row of swings. The woman was pushing a blond little boy and nodded at Lena's son Cosmo, who was even blonder. She asked in their language how long Lena had been his babysitter.

Oh no, he's my son, Lena said. She'd become accustomed to strangers making this assumption and turned the conversation away from her with her usual onslaught of questions. The woman with the braid responded to each inquiry in an eerily steady voice, as if she'd been waiting for them. Across the three swings that hung empty between them, she told Lena she'd come after dropping out of college. She was taller, with long, elegant arms and a sharp, knowing gaze, which she kept fixed on Lena with an unnerving boldness. Lena felt the woman taking in every aspect of her, not just her mouth and eyes, but the width of her hips beneath her baggy, unflattering pants, the air of resigned sexlessness she had about her since she'd become a mother.

The blond boy in the other swing kicked his legs and urged the woman with the braid to push him higher, and the woman did with the same transfixing steadiness, telling Lena as she pushed him that she had studied engineering on the island but was thinking about going for a bachelor's here in something else. But first she needed to save up more money and improve her comprehension of the language. I keep meaning to take a class, she told Lena, but I come home so tired.

The woman jutted her chin in the direction of the little boy in the swing, and Lena nodded, confessing she had vastly underestimated the amount of rereading she'd have to do to get through grad school in another language—and on her own with a child. She told the woman with the braid that she had come with her son for a PhD in education but felt delirious at night, trying to write papers after getting Cosmo into bed and finishing the dishes. I know it will look like an act of defeat, but I'm thinking of heading back to the island after completing the master's, she admitted, and see if I can get a job with the Ministry of Education. It was a confession she'd yet to make aloud to anyone.

The last of the summer humidity still had not lifted, and in the languid air of the playground Lena began to feel sweat forming under her arms as the other woman replied that she, too, hoped to go back to the island—eventually. She told Lena that before she dropped out of college, she'd gotten caught up in the protests against rising tuition and the outrageous salaries the university deans were taking. I stopped handing in assignments, and then other things got complicated, the woman added, a hardness taking over her face.

In the swing, Cosmo wailed for Lena to push him again. She thrust her hands out without looking, scraping her knuckles against the plastic back of the seat. She swore at the sting and then about her constant exhaustion. If you ever need help on the weekends, the woman offered, I could give you my number.

A faint breeze moved through the playground then, trembling the leaves in the tall row of trees behind them. The breeze carried the colder air of autumn, and Lena felt the brisk press of it against the back of her legs and neck as she pulled out her cell phone. The woman recited her number in the same commanding, steady voice and Lena punched it into her phone, a metal clamp closing over her chest as she waited for the name.

I'm Maria, the woman said at last. And you?

Freddy peered down at the bundled-up northerners hustling along the sidewalk below with their dogs and groceries. His friend's street looked just like the one from a comedy about this neighborhood that everyone on the island had watched when he was a child. The family in the comedy had lived on a posh street lined with the same leafy trees, the same cement staircases leading up to the imposing wooden doors of each building.

He still couldn't quite grasp that a play of his was actually going to open in four days in this most revered city in the hemisphere. It was astounding how much one's prospects could change with proximity to a serious cash flow. All it had taken was for a close friend to marry a banker here and he was no longer a provincial playwright stuck in the same crumbling port city where he was born.

At last, he was more than just fat old Freddy with the sparkle scarf at the Zodiac. More than the younger gay brother the senator rarely mentioned. He was international now. His friend had hired a translator and professional actors. She had scheduled a premier date in October because she believed good things happened for shows that opened in October.

Standing across from him, next to the hum of her gleaming state-of-the-art dishwasher, his friend was washing some grapes to eat with the overpriced cheese she'd bought with her banker husband's endless influx of money. Freddy clicked on the electric kettle for their tea and looked out the window again, still astounded that he was actually here, on a classy street just like the one on the comedy they'd all watched as if it were a myth.

I know there are more people from the island we could invite, his friend said from the sink. Oh, you know who else lives here now? Ugh, I can't remember her name. Her family owns Sunny Juice and she had a kid with a tourist. You know who I'm talking about, right? Don't you know her from something?

Freddy lifted his hand above the now steaming spout of the kettle. Yes, he said, Lena. He let the wet burn of the steam spread over his open palm and waited for the heat to reveal where the first blister might begin.

For weeks after the play about his father opened at the Zodiac, he'd considered calling Lena to say he'd seen the vicious way his brother had seized her wrist. He'd wanted to tell her he had also asked about Maria P., over and over, and would have continued to ask if Victor hadn't stopped answering his calls. He hadn't spoken to his brother until the wedding nearly a year later, when Freddy saw his sister-in-law was already pregnant.

The day after his nephew was born, he'd gone over and Victor had insisted he hold the baby. Everyone had joked the boy had Victor's chin, which was the same chin as their mother. Freddy had found the baby's squirming close-eyed innocence overwhelming. He hadn't known what to say after Victor announced the baby's name would be Edgar, for their uncle. Freddy felt their shared history fall over him, silent as a bedsheet. You'd better keep each other alive, their father had warned the two of them at breakfast and often again at dinner. You'll amount to nothing if you don't.

When Freddy returned home after holding his nephew, he locked all of his Future Candidate scenes in a drawer.

Victor sat up a little taller with the pleasure of perusing so many potential slogans about himself. His new press secretary had just delivered the list.

A SENATOR OF DECISIVE ACTION

He liked the catchy yet serious tone of that one. And he was remarkably decisive, wasn't he? He'd brought on this new press secretary earlier in the year and was more than pleased with her so far. She was Jewish and savvy. She wasn't bad looking either, once he'd gotten used to the narrowness of her face. Under the slogan, she'd written a note about building on the idea by dropping in the words decisive and action during his interviews. Oh, she was definitely savvy, this Sara, and on top of that she had the relentless drive he often found among others who'd had a relative rounded up and disappeared. Sara had lost an aunt of hers. Victor couldn't recall the aunt's name, although it was really his business to know such things—the girl worked for him.

Victor sucked in his gut and left his office, beyond which lay the exhilarating sight of his half-dozen employees all hunched over their keyboards, tapping away on his behalf. In the far corner, Sara was working intently, her dark curly hair twisted up into a plastic clip. He liked a girl unafraid to pull her hair back and expose her face.

On the edge of Sara's desk, he planted his hand and drummed his fingers against the laminate. I just wanted to come over and thank you, he said. You really nailed it: a candidate of decisive action. It's absolutely brilliant.

Sara lifted her face and he saw that his compliment had endowed her brown eyes with a glassy shine. Pleased with himself, he planted his other hand on the back of her chair and asked if she could join him for lunch to talk some more about the slogan. I was trying to remember the name of your aunt, he said—what was her name again?

Exact same as mine, Sara said, with a plaintive tilt of her head. Even her last name. She was my father's sister.

Victor let his gut slacken and expand over the confines of his belt. I named my son for my uncle, too, he said, bearing down more weight on the back of Sara's chair. Every time he thought of little Edgar, his whole body went soft in a way that felt insurmountable. So what do you say to lunch? he asked, bending a little closer to her face. You hungry?

Oscar and his wife liked to throw around the word *abomination*. Every time they came to this renowned uptown hospital for an ultrasound they agreed the narrow waiting room chairs on the obstetrics floor were a complete abomination. On most things, they agreed with an almost hypnotic ease. No plastic toys for their new daughter. No pacifiers or crying it out. They both wanted the baby to be in the care of a parent for at least the first six months and agreed that, financially, it made the most sense for it to be Oscar, who could resume the baking classes he taught at several schools and senior centers the following winter.

Oscar doubted picking up a full schedule of classes again would be that simple, but he wanted to begin fatherhood right, to place his own interests last in a way he wished his father had been more willing to do. By email, his father had already postponed his trip to meet the baby because of some cruise with his girlfriend. With a sigh, Oscar picked up the copy of *Get Out*, the city's nightlife and events magazine, lying on the waiting room table. Beside him, his wife was reading a pamphlet about cord blood banking, though they'd already agreed it wasn't their sort of thing, and they couldn't afford it anyway.

Oscar flipped indolently through the film reviews and then skipped ahead, past the stand-up comedy pages, to the theater listings, where he stopped, his mind blaring like an ambulance at the third listing. *Where He Danced While We Lay Dreaming*. Beneath was the play's name in the original language and a thumbnail-sized photograph of a man spinning with a feather boa around his neck.

He reread the description to be certain, the blare more piercing now, and he thought maybe it wasn't internal after all, but coming from outside the hospital, the sound carrying up from the busy avenue below.

The blare went on pressing forward in his brain until he could feel the pressure of it against the back of his eyes. It was definitely internal. It was anguish, the blare of regret.

Oscar dropped the magazine onto his wife's lap to get it away from himself. I saw this play once, he tapped the listing, when I was traveling. It has tango in it. You'd probably like it.

His wife lifted the magazine over the protrusion of her stomach and agreed she loved tango. I always forget you did that backpacking thing, she said. You never talk about it.

Oscar agreed that was true, it didn't come up much, did it? He leaned his head back against the wall so his wife wouldn't see how intently he was shutting his eyes. There was no reason for her to suspect that somewhere inside him he might still be standing on a hill outside another woman's house in another country, wondering what might have happened if they'd first slept together a week earlier, if they'd had even one extra day to work through their assumptions about each other before the shock of sitting in front of that ancient TV and watching his country being attacked. No matter how many times he went over it, he couldn't figure out why it had felt so necessary to lash out at Lena for biting into her scone.

He'd read much more about the island since living there, about the torture techniques his country had imparted to the island's military. He'd skimmed endless articles online about the lack of transparency, even now, about the full role his country had played in the fraudulent vote that had put the regime in power. He'd grown chagrined at how little history he'd taken in his four semesters of college before switching to culinary school. After he met his wife, even well into their marriage, whenever he saw a mention of the island, the thought of the way he had berated Lena caused a tremor of self-loathing to quake in him.

Around him in the waiting room now, the air felt increasingly thin and inadequate. Beside him, his wife asked if he wanted to order tickets to the play and he said yes.

SCENES TO BE INCINERATED
(WORK IN PROGRESS BY ANONYMOUS)

Early in the twenty-first century.

Country undefined.

SET

Downstage, a cardboard ranch house floats just above the floor.

Upstage, a shiny question mark floats above head height.

The question mark should shimmer notably in the stage light.

The senator's brother enters.

Without acknowledging the shiny question mark,

he comes to a stop beneath it.

The senator's son skips onto the stage.

He stops beside his uncle and looks up.

SENATOR'S SON

Uncle, is Father sitting in a pen full of stinky pigs?

SENATOR'S BROTHER

Why would you ask such a thing, Nephew? What's led you
to wonder if he might be sitting in a stinky pen?

SENATOR'S SON

The pigs are okay in there, right?

SENATOR'S BROTHER

Well, we certainly hope so, don't we?

SENATOR'S SON

And why does Father have such a big, lumpy backpack on?
What's in there?

SENATOR'S BROTHER

What is in there, eh? Why is it so many people who go into
politics end up hauling around such big, lumpy backpacks
like that?

SENATOR'S SON

Why do you always answer with questions,
Uncle?

SENATOR'S BROTHER

Why do you always ask me questions?

SENATOR'S SON

Because you always have a shiny question mark floating over your head when you come to see us.

The brother looks up.

He has to crane his neck to see the question mark.

SENATOR'S BROTHER

I guess I do, don't I?

On the train to the party for Freddy, Lena tried to get through the essay she'd been assigned for Monday. The author kept referring to "the strange masks" of humanity in other cultures. She assumed the author was using the phrase ironically. Even in this most dominant of countries, she didn't think a widely read author in the twenty-first century could still earnestly refer to the humanity of other cultures as masked and strange. Unless, perhaps, they still did.

She turned the essay over on her lap and leaned her head against the train window behind her. On weekend afternoons, she rarely went anywhere without Cosmo, and the oddness of being in transit alone on a Saturday had slowed her thoughts down, condensing them into a heavy haze. As the train tunneled below the city, she felt wistful for the teetering diesel buses of her island. She missed the shared cabs and random intimacy of cramming into the backseat with two strangers, taking in the ocean together after every few turns in the road.

She felt trapped traveling everywhere in this city underground, watching nothing but a smear of darkness and graffiti outside the grimy windows of the train.

Her longing only increased when she reached the building where the party was taking place and heard one of her favorite bands from the island playing inside. The door was unlocked and Freddy's spectacular booming laugh floated up from the back patio. The barbecue had begun at two with the idea of hanging out all afternoon before heading to the play, but Lena hadn't wanted to leave Cosmo for that many hours in a row. She'd finally found a babysitter they both liked, a younger sister of one of her classmates. The girl had been their salvation during the weeks when Cosmo got one virus after another. Lena hadn't been able to stay on top of her assignments. At night, Cosmo kept calling for her and vomiting on the bed. In her Friday seminar, during a discussion on the cognitive benefits of word problems, she'd had to hold her eyelids up with her thumbs to stay awake.

As she stepped alone into the apartment, it struck her how deeply bewildering and lonely those nights had been, continually checking Cosmo's temperature, changing his pajamas, lying awake beside him, terrified that she wasn't doing enough. Arriving this late to the party, all the drunk, joking voices drifting up from the back patio sounded imposing and intimidating. In the first doorway, she spotted a desk chair draped with coats and purses in what looked like a home office. But once she stepped inside to leave her bag, she realized the room was much deeper than it looked from the hall and it wasn't empty of people, as she'd assumed. At the back, there was a black futon with a woman seated on it, straddling the lap of a man who had his fingers in her hair.

Lena apologized and started to back out of the room until the woman turned and Lena stiffened, recognizing the woman's steady, knowing gaze immediately.

Hey, the woman said in a murmur so low it bordered on sensual. I'm Maria, remember? I was waiting to hear from you.

Lena opened her mouth but couldn't think what to respond. She'd never called after meeting in the playground. Everything about the encounter had felt too fraught, though she had kept the number on her phone and continued to replay the conversation, to question whether the resemblance to Maria P. was as strong as it had felt at the time.

I meant to call, she said, watching as Maria slowly extracted herself one leg at a time from the man's lap. The young man got up then as well, his face difficult to make out in the unlit room. But as they both moved toward her, something about him felt potently familiar to her, too. The confidence in his gaze, his slight swagger as he drew closer. Or was it the green soccer jersey he had on from the best-known team on the island, the same jersey her brothers and all the boys she'd ever dated had worn to the games. When he leaned over to kiss her cheek, Lena leaned toward him enough to feel his stubble against her face.

Lena and I met a little while ago, Maria said in the same low, yet forceful whisper.

I think maybe we've met before, too, haven't we? the boy said in a similarly liquid, illicit way.

Lena wondered if they'd taken Ecstasy. When one of their hands lightly brushed her own, she twitched. It had been so long since a hand felt that electric against her palm. Startled at her own reaction, Lena didn't look down to see which of them the fingers belonged to, whose hand briefly reached up then and brushed her hair from her face—a touch so soft and water-like that she released a sound as faint and hollowed out as the wind's over the open mouth of a bottle.

With Maria standing this close, with her eerily similar height and narrow face, Lena could not settle on whether this woman was an apparition or someone else entirely, who'd just happened to leave the island the same year. Lena didn't know if her uncertainty was the cause of her stillness, or if it was the sickening lack of motion she still felt when she came across a mention of Victor, or met anyone named Maria. Or the sense of immobility that came over her when the payments arrived each month from her parents, causing her to replay the Sundays again, her grandfather defending Cato, the endless clack of the juice bottles moving tyrannically through the conveyor belts of her family's factory—all the caught things inside her straining to be released.

And couldn't something at least be resolved in the silence of a small room, in the accepting of an uncertain hand in an uncertain place? By the time Maria's lips brushed her cheek in what was a greeting or far more than that, it all felt inevitable—the dark office and their three bodies inside it, drawing closer in a country that belonged to none of them.

Freddy was determined not to reveal his disappointment. In the photos his friend sent of the theater she'd found for his play, the large stone building had looked like an impressive venue for a theatrical debut. His friend had never mentioned the building was on a random avenue surrounded by car washes and warehouses. He hadn't realized until he'd arrived and come to watch the rehearsals that the building was on a soulless thoroughfare a long train ride away from the downtown theater world where he'd imagined the play would be performed.

His friend assured him people paid attention to the shows there anyhow. She said his play had been listed in the city's main events magazine and people would come. He knew only an ungrateful, insatiable narcissist would sulk in the entryway like this, standing apart from everyone on the opening night of his debut in this most auspicious of cities, still regretting and obsessing about the venue. And he was pleased with the actors. The translator was married to a man from the island and had done what seemed like an excellent job for next to nothing.

Let it go, Freddy told himself. He'd had over a week to let it go, yet even now, he could not stop wishing the green tiling wasn't so badly chipped in the entryway. The wiring backstage was as much of a tangled firetrap as at the Zodiac.

With a sigh, Freddy clutched at his good luck scarf and wished he'd had more wine.

He'd been too nervous to say much at all to Lena. He hadn't seen her in the backyard until the very end of the gathering, after some irritating young couple had come down and taken food and left without any interest in seeing the play. He looked around for Lena in the lobby and spotted her among some of the people from the barbecue now clustered near the ticket booth. He hoped someone who wasn't connected to his country or related to the actors would walk in soon. It was astounding how many ways an opening night could collapse into a series of disappointments.

As he crossed toward the ticket booth, he saw Lena's expression abruptly change and guessed it must be in response to the anxiety on his face. He forced a more confident smile in her direction and hoped he looked less conflicted. But Lena didn't react and Freddy realized she wasn't responding because her gaze was on someone else, someone behind him. It occurred to him Lena might have come late after debating whether to come at all. Most likely she felt nothing for him at this point but resentment and assumed that whatever he knew about Maria he'd never betray Victor. And wasn't she right?

One night, as a kid, he'd heard a strange, high-pitched sound and come down to find his father drunk and weeping, slumped against the wall across from the photo that hung in the entryway of lanky ten-year-old Edgar with his arm around their father. When he told Victor the next morning, Victor admitted he'd heard the same sound another night and found their father slumped in front of the picture, too. Victor had insisted they needed to be that committed to each other as well. Even when there's nothing left, Victor said, you can't let go of your brother.

Lena watched Oscar reel back at the sight of her. She watched him clutch the arm of the pregnant woman at his side, who was such an equivalent shade of blond they looked like siblings. When Oscar finally reached her and introduced his wife, Lena nodded, waiting for him to say her name to his wife, but he didn't. He just busied himself making an exaggerated chivalrous fuss of assisting his pregnant wife out of her coat. Underneath the coat, the wife had on a loose satin maternity shirt. The satin was a cream color, almost beige. In the cheap fluorescent lighting it took on a sheen that accentuated the curve of her profile. The expectant mother with the proud, protective father at her side.

So, the wife said in a loud, confident voice, I'm guessing you two know each other from Oscar's backpacking days?

Oscar, still clutching his wife's coat like a life jacket, nodded and said, Yes, we met in a used bookstore, though it mostly sold pot.

His wife let out a little ironic laugh at this, which Oscar immediately echoed. At their conspiratorial laughter, Lena felt her legs weakening, an unsteadiness rising into her chest and up into her head. Since she'd arrived in this country, the Sublime had taken on an air of holiness in her mind—the freeing absence of judgment she had felt there with Olga, nursing Cosmo and inventing humorous roles for him in future revolutions, the joyful relief she'd felt every time she walked in and collapsed on the sunken couch in Conspiracy.

In an amused voice, Oscar's wife asked her if she'd worked there, at this place fronting as a bookstore.

It wasn't just a front, Lena said and looked over at Oscar to correct his wife and explain what a defiantly revolutionary place the

Sublime was. But he just stood there staring back at her with an agonized expression, his eyes making it plain that seeing her again was causing him torment. If the current world order had not gone up in flames that morning—or if it had, but their gut reaction had not been to attack each other—Lena wondered if maybe her son might have grown up with a father.

Well, whatever the store really was, his wife said, her hands coming together protectively in front of the curve of her shimmering satin shirt, I hope you've been able to find better work here.

Lena emitted a flat, ironic laugh in response. She wanted nothing more than to get away from them, but knew it was possible she may never find herself standing in front of her son's father again.

You know, she said, I should get your email, Oscar.

Freddy waited till the blond couple had moved toward the ticket window before he drew up and looped his arm through Lena's. Did you invite those blond people? he asked.

You could put it that way, Lena said with finality as another northerner stepped into the theater, a tall bald man with bad posture and glasses and what seemed like the confident air of an important critic. Freddy tried to repress the birdlike flutter of hope in his chest, to ignore the growing commotion of it and keep his focus on Lena beside him. But what if this hunched-over, bespectacled man was indeed from the most revered paper in this most revered of cultural cities?

With Lena beside him, the intensity of his desire for a major critic here to approve of his work felt shallow and absurd. But this city's paper had been the gateway for every recent playwright on the island whose work had gotten out. A review here made all the other destinies that much easier to reach.

Isn't it maddening, he said, his arm still through Lena's, all of us hoping to get something out of this country that's orchestrated how many horror shows all over this hemisphere?

It is obscenely maddening. Lena cast her eyes around the entryway at the clusters of people around them, the vast majority of them from their island.

A strange thing happened to me in that little office at your friend's house, where the coats were, Lena said, still facing away from him. There was a woman in it who looked eerily like Maria P. You know who I'm talking about, right? Lena turned to him now. The student who died on Trinity Hill? Lena paused, averted her gaze a moment. Your brother nearly choked me to death once, she said. Over a flyer I lost.

Freddy keeled slightly toward her. Victor told me he panicked about the flyer. But, Freddy said, the way Victor told it, that was all.

From *The Islander*

Fight for Repeal of Amnesty Law Continues

. . . Among the senators pushing for a repeal of the amnesty law protecting military and correctional personnel from being tried for crimes under Cato is the port's own senator, Victor M. . . .

"Until we prosecute every single person who got away with murder in this country," the senator said, "we can't move forward as a society. Families deserve the truth. We all deserve the truth. How can anyone move on without the truth?"

On the stage, once again, a man spun with nothing in his arms but a feathered red boa. With each turn he made, all the feathers lifted and reddened the air around him. The tendons went taut in his neck as he tilted his head back, exaggerating the distance between himself and the feathered red proxy in his arms.

But only for a moment.

At the next spin, the man clutched the boa to his chest again. Oscar watched even more breathlessly than the first time how conflicted the man looked as he turned in furious circles about the stage. Endless turns which resolved nothing.

How was a father—how was anyone—supposed to know who to be true to at any given moment? In giving Lena an erroneous email address in the lobby, had he been cowardly and deceitful? Or had it been a necessary act, what any loyal, chivalrous husband with a pregnant wife would do?

He had felt his wife's shoulders relax under his arm as he'd recited the numbers of his long-defunct first college ID. Ok65, he had repeated, watching Lena's delicate fingers move over the screen of her phone. He'd felt no choice but to show his loyalty, to be true to his seven-month-pregnant wife. Hadn't that been what had destroyed his parents' marriage, failing to remain true to each other before anyone or anything else?

If he'd come alone, or with a friend, Oscar was certain he would have been able to say more, to ask Lena about what had brought her to the city, and about Olga. He would have rambled his way to expressing his regret at not seeing her again before he left the island. After fleeing Lena's, he'd done nothing but sit in his hostel listening to the updates get worse and worse. He'd left the island less than a week later, without finishing the classes he'd already paid for at the language school.

More than once, while molding scones or washing trays, he'd thought about what he might say to Lena if he ever saw her again. To imagine the elaborate explanations and apologies he would offer to her had filled him with a sense of decency, and relief.

The thought that he would never have to see Lena and actually say them had filled him with relief as well.

In the dark, while the father on stage went on maniacally spinning with his contradictions and his ring of feathers, Oscar reached over and placed his hand on his wife's thigh. The theater had no permanent seats, only rows of cheap folding chairs with the thinnest of cushions. He murmured to his wife that the seats were abominable and asked her if she was uncomfortable.

I think we both know I'm uncomfortable, don't we, Oscar? she murmured back and moved her leg away. If you only knew that woman for a few days, why would she ask for your email when you're clearly married and expecting a baby?

I honestly don't know, I swear. Oscar lifted his eyes again to the stage. Three other actors had emerged with feathered boas and were beginning to turn in sync with the father. Oscar didn't recall anyone else joining this scene the first time. The others had come on later, after the intermission. Or had the others been there from the beginning and he just didn't remember, having been so riveted by the father?

Onstage, sweat was trickling down the father's temples now and gleaming on his chin. Stains had darkened his underarms and the front of his thin shirt. Swift and hard, over and over, the father extended one of his feet out a few inches then slid it back to meet his other foot. Then he took another step, slightly wider, then a smaller one. With an emphatic stomp, the whole ambivalent sequence repeated—his leg extending out only to slide back. Out. Back. Stomp. Faster. As if the father had lost all control of his own feet.

The drilling across the street began at exactly six a.m., the sound blasting into every dream of every slumbering being for blocks around. Nowhere on the island had Lena ever heard a drill shattering through concrete at this hour. It was uncivilized.

As occurred every morning, seconds after the aural assault of the drilling started up, a small creature in leaf-print pajamas bounded into her room and pressed its cold nose against her forehead. Hello, my favorite mother, the creature said.

Hello, my favorite offspring. She raised the bedcover for the creature to burrow down beside her. The warmth of Cosmo's small body against her own felt protective, a fortress she could seal herself behind anytime, even after the shock of seeing Oscar. Although maybe it was terrible of her to covet her child as a fortress—proof that some part of her still longed for the walls she had grown up behind.

She thought of her mother just before she'd left the island, trailing her to the wrought-iron gate that was the only way out of her parents' compound, asking why Lena was compelled to make life so difficult for herself.

You're not going to change the world, Lena, her mother had declared, by moving alone with a baby to another country. Your real problem, her mother insisted, her voice strident and rising, is not the judgment of anyone else on this island. It's that you can't stop judging yourself. That's your real problem, and it always has been. Your family didn't kill anyone. I've never understood what you're so ashamed of.

As her mother shouted, Lena had yanked on the gate to release herself and Cosmo onto the street in front of her parents' house. But the latch on the gate was sticking from the heat and her mother just stood with crossed arms and watched her struggle. Lena tried to jangle the latch harder while balancing Cosmo on her hip, clutching him as intensely as if she were clutching humanity itself.

No, she didn't want Oscar or anyone questioning how she chose to raise her child.

Come closer, she said to her one and only under the covers. I'm cold.

Victor counted the open mouths of the zeroes on the check from his cousin. He hadn't been expecting another donation check. It had arrived as unbidden as the odor of pig shit. The way they'd set things up, his cousin was to receive four consultant fees and then send a portion of the total sum along to Victor as a donation for his reelection campaign. There wasn't supposed to be a second donation check. It was hush money and his cousin should have known better than to cash anything unexpected with the national news reporting now on the smell.

But people near the factory had to be exaggerating. The flow of waste couldn't possibly be enough to have formed an entire lake of fecal sludge. Grandmothers weren't actually fainting from the odor. Whatever people placed on their tongues couldn't actually taste of pigs. Children weren't really beginning to snort at school and root around in the mud. And now, the parents of four teenagers hospitalized for nausea and dizziness after bathing in a nearby pond were insisting the cause was the factory runoff reaching the pond underground.

You told me people did this sort of consultant fee all the time and no one cared, his cousin shouted at him on the phone, and Victor assured him they were going to resolve the problem. Although in truth he did not see how they would, and if there was anyone who was going to end up jobless over the debacle it would be his cousin, whose name was on every inspection report. His cousin was the one who had received checks from the farm as an independent agricultural consultant. Victor had assured him the arrangement was no big deal. He'd promised his cousin government employees often augmented their salary with consultant fees though no one talked about it, which was true. What Victor had not mentioned was that such an arrangement was technically against the law, while his receiving a donation from his cousin was not.

Over the weekend, he'd thought about going to see his cousin but decided a visit would only invite more accusations. The previous week his cousin had emailed a photo of the vast brown expanse of porcine piss and waste behind the factory, though Victor had told him not to send anything by email. He had never seen that much sludgy, crusted shit in one place. It was indeed lake-size. Just looking at it, Victor could imagine how vile the smell must get with the heat in the interior, how the odor would just keep growing fouler and traveling farther every day.

For his cousin to be dull-witted enough to deposit an unexpected check this large and send on another donation struck Victor as astoundingly naïve. Or maybe his cousin knew he was going to get fired anyhow and decided he might as well cash in on this last sum while he could.

I have someone looking out for your cousin. He won't get fired, Victor's father-in-law had assured him. *Neither of you are going to be exposed or blamed for this.*

His father-in-law, however, had also promised that his inept friend, the owner, was getting the situation under control, that the factory had just bought a top-of-the-line industrial filter. His father-in-law hadn't mentioned that the filter was equipped to handle the waste of a mere five thousand animals. Not forty thousand.

That morning the island's main tabloid had run a spoof, printing swine-shaped clouds floating across the rural middle of the island. It was only a matter of time before the papers would figure out who was to blame. They would start with his cousin but it wouldn't end there. Sara had already come to him about some journalist with a stutter asking for his comments on the situation. The journalist had noticed the owner was an old private school friend of a certain venerable senator, and the name on all the inspections was a man with the same last name as his son-in-law, known for his mesmerizing speeches on the importance of exposing the truth.

Victor had called the owner and threatened to go and cut the pigs' throats himself if they weren't all slaughtered within the week. The whole thing had become an all-you-can-eat dinner buffet for the media. Victor didn't see what choice he had but to let his cousin take the fall at this point.

He folded the check and tucked it into his wallet. Sara would be savvy enough to deflect the questions somehow. They'd move past it. Decisively. To reap the rewards of the world, a man had to learn how to move forward at any cost. It was the relentless questioners like his brother who got stuck and failed. Of course it was.

SCENES TO BE INCINERATED
(WORK IN PROGRESS BY ANONYMOUS)

SET

To the left, a suspended cardboard statue of Socrates.

To the right, a heap of laundry.

The senator and his brother stroll onto the stage together.

They are sipping beers.

The senator passes the statue and keeps on walking.

His brother stops next to it.

SENATOR'S BROTHER

You walked right past my Socrates.

SENATOR

Your who?

SENATOR'S BROTHER

My new Socrates—"Be as you wish to seem."

I'm writing about his proverb.

His followers say he adhered to it.

But maybe they just didn't know him that well.

Maybe Socrates was secretly a hypocrite.

SENATOR

And who cares if he adhered to it?

He's still Socrates.

He's got playwrights cutting out crude statues of him instead of doing something about their laundry.

When was the last time you washed any of the pants here, in this heap?

The senator's brother turns and addresses the statue.

SENATOR'S BROTHER

Tell him, Socrates, tell my brother how much that proverb came to haunt you. I bet you were quietly horrified at your private capacity for hypocrisy, weren't you?

SENATOR

I can't believe you're interrogating a piece of cardboard.

You need to get out more, brother.

You need to wash your pants and go eat in a restaurant.

The statue of Socrates begins to spin.

*It swings left and then right and then more wildly around
the stage.*

A commanding male voice, issuing Socratic proverbs in Greek,

emanates from the speakers.

As the Godlike voice drones on,

the brother pursues the swinging Socrates across the stage.

The brother's pursuit should include a range of movements.

One move like an elephant, another like Baryshnikov.

The swinging statue should hit the senator at least once.

The two brothers could collide as well.

Whatever happens,

the senator should remain impervious.

After minutes of escalating absurdity,

the brother trips over his own laundry.

He falls.

The statue comes to a halt as well.

Expressionless, the senator polishes off his beer.

He exits alone.

Olga felt the least capable of being alive when it was overcast. If she had to head up the stairs to the store under a mass of clouds, she would find herself longing most acutely for a heart attack, or an aneurysm—anything to get it over with already.

Occasionally, however, there would be a morning as clear as this one, with such an abundance of crisp early light accompanying her up the crumbling steps to the Sublime that she couldn't help feeling irrefutably among the living. The recent boom in the island's economy had been moving books off the shelves at an unprecedented rate of two a day, and her dope sales had gone through the roof. She'd finally fixed the pipes in the bathroom and bought a used computer off her journalist friend Simon. With Lena gone, she let Simon stammer on to her about his investigations as much as he wanted. He kept her internet working and she couldn't fathom going without it again. She rarely opened her transaction log now. It was so much easier to zone out and click her life away, bingeing on the infinite sickening reports about everywhere.

Now that the toilet was fixed, she could sip tea until she'd skimmed all the disasters and scandals she could bear. Victor the Invincible was in the national news again with that grim, confident stare of his. She was just about to scroll down past his likeness when a name in the caption pricked her vision like a needle.

She lifted her fingers to the screen, bewildered. She was imagining it. The name wasn't there. In the photo, half-concealed behind Victor, there was no sliver of a young woman with S's thick hair. S's dark eyes. No thin plastic mattress. No soldier forcing her into the corner while the rest of them were led out.

Not long after dawn, Victor stepped onto the balcony off the master bedroom with his son. The mist had not yet lifted from the manicured lawn around their new oceanfront apartment. Beyond the lawn, fog obscured the water. Victor heard his wife calling from the bedroom that it was too cold for Edgar to be outside in pajamas, but Victor just slid the balcony door shut. Every morning Cristina yelled at him about something. Tired of it, he'd been coming home later in the evening, which meant the morning was his only time with Edgar. What did it matter if the boy wore his pajamas outside?

We're street dogs, aren't we? He grinned at his boy. A little chill isn't going to kill a street dog. You don't want to grow up into a little pampered poodle, do you?

Edgar shook his head and said he did not, though the boy had wrapped his scrawny arms over his chest. He had curled his bare toes against the cold concrete of the balcony and then Victor heard the click begin of his son's little milk teeth chattering against each other, his whole scrawny body quaking with shivers. Victor had no recollection of being that weak and prone to girlish trembling when he and Freddy snuck out together in the morning and peed on the trees.

At the thought, Victor grabbed his son's skinny, quivering arm. If you wanted to, he warned his son, I bet you could stop making that noise with your teeth.

But beneath his father's grip, Edgar went on chattering and trembling, as dramatic as his mother. Before Victor even realized what he was doing, he shoved the boy backward. The sliding glass door of the balcony rattled as Edgar fell against it. A stiff terror took over the boy's small face, and Victor looked away from him. Go on, he said, yanking the door open, get in there.

Without a word Edgar slipped inside and Victor found himself alone again, the only street dog in his household. Oh how he abhorred his wife's family and their fussy bourgeois obsession with appearances. He abhorred them more every minute. He hadn't told his father-in-law or Cristina before his drive yesterday out to the pig farm. Somebody had to grab that lying bastard who had caused all the problems and tell him to drain that shit pond or he was going to find himself floating in it facedown. Trying to pay more people off was just postponing a solution. They needed to slaughter the pigs. There wasn't time to separate the ones healthy enough to sell for meat. The odor had been viler than Victor had expected. He'd been able to smell it, the reek of feces emanating from his clothes, the whole drive home.

Wrapping his palms over the chilly metal of the balcony railing, he leaned out over the misted lawn. The fog had begun to lift from the ocean, revealing some debris in the water swirling toward the shoreline. It looked like a large slab of cardboard, or the broken-off panel of a boat. Nobody was even trying to control the trash problem around the island. Every morning tide now carried debris toward his building, some unsightly object drifting closer, determined to wreck his view.

Lena opened the link in Olga's email. The sight of Victor's stiff, deliberate smile caused a swift, cold numbness down her spine, as total as an epidural. The longer Lena had been gone from the island, the easier it had become to resist opening articles about Victor. It had been months since she had opened even one.

She had never heard Olga speak of anyone she'd been detained with, let alone a Sara who had been the love of her life. As for the young press secretary beside Victor in the photograph, Olga was right. She was beaming at him as admiringly as Maria P.

I had no idea my Sara had a niece with her name, Olga had written amid her repeated adamant requests for Lena to write to this young Sara immediately at the email Olga had found for her. But what if Olga's concern for this young woman was misplaced?

Olga explained that she had already written to Sara herself. *But it will be more powerful for her to hear it from you directly,* Olga went on in her email, adding that she had a plan in mind already, both to get Sara out of his office and *to get that bastard. Tell her about Maria P.,* Olga ordered; *tell her about him nearly killing you.*

Lena closed the link to get rid of Victor's face. It had taken her so long to stop returning constantly to the thought of him. But in the decade she and Olga had now been friends, she could not recall a single request Olga had ever made of her. And what risk was Olga really asking her to take? If Sara found the email inappropriate, even hysterical, if she read it with scorn, if she forwarded it to Victor and asked if he knew this unhinged woman emailing with such outlandish accusations, what did it matter? What could Victor do to her with a whole ocean between them?

And it was such a small risk, next to the possibility that she might prevent some other young woman from becoming the next Maria P. dead on a road—or, like herself, having to remember, for years, the sound of her own gasping until the world dimmed inward, the terror of waking up limp on the floor, still alone with Victor, his tense body hovering over her.

For Olga, for Maria P., Lena drew closer to the keyboard at the hallway computer stand outside her seminar room and forced herself to tap out the words. She purged everything that happened in the basement—including the minutes she had yet to confide even to Olga, the ones after she regained consciousness, when she had numbly stayed on in the basement. Victor had asked if she was all right, but made no other acknowledgment of what he had done beyond speaking in a lower, more hesitant tone about the next march. Sitting slightly farther away from him than usual, she had gone right on listening.

It was not until she boarded a bus home that she had touched the painful spots on her throat where he'd dug in his fingers the hardest. She still felt stunned at the number of minutes she had remained there, listening to him, before making her way up the basement stairs and on through his family's kitchen to the front door, still disturbed at the full day it had taken her to recognize that she would never place herself in a room with Victor again.

Without rereading the email to Sara, she pressed send. She held in her breath. Then let it go. She had not just stewed and cringed this time, scolding herself with the punishing thought that no other young woman could be nearly as naïve and shame-ridden as she had been.

All through her 9:45 a.m. seminar, as her classmates debated the possible pedagogical merit of video games for reluctant readers, she stared out at the leaves churning in the wind outside before allowing herself to glance back at the clock on the wall, recalculating the minutes until she could check her email again.

But after her seminar there was no response from Sara. And nothing more from Olga either.

On her train home, pressed against too many strangers barreling together underground, Lena remained standing, watching the darkness flickering by outside the windows. She thought about Olga never mentioning a beloved even once, at least not to her. Lena could not recall Olga confiding about anyone detained with her or any details of that time at all. Lena had assumed that limit to their friendship had to do with her family and had never pried. With sorrow, she realized Olga had probably confided now solely out of necessity.

Coming up from the train, Lena checked her mail again. Nothing from Sara. Nothing from Olga.

She picked her son up from day care, boiled chicken drumsticks for their dinner, and thought about the mistrust that is the legacy of a divide, how much safer it felt to withhold anything close to trust in a country as bitterly divided as her own.

She warmed the water for her son's bath, steaming up their tiny bathroom until she could no longer see her face in the mirror.

At last, after getting her son in bed and sweeping his bits of chicken off the floor, after multiple waves of deepening doubt and self-pity and bitterly concluding that women did not want random strangers reaching out with emotional warnings, unloading some fraught history they had no reason to believe or care about, Sara's reply arrived not from the Senate but from a personal email.

Lena skimmed through the thank-you and statements of commiseration: . . . *had to invent a boyfriend for him to stop . . . but again at lunch . . . his arm . . . started to question . . . yet stayed on . . . his fight for the amnesty laws . . . having been named for an aunt who . . . about to meet Olga . . . emboldened after hearing from you both . . . want to do something . . . perhaps you have heard on the news here . . . the vile smell . . .*

Two hours before they'd agreed to meet, Olga took a bus down to Independence Square. She had not told Sara why she had chosen such an old, run-down sandwich shop. For forty years, Olga had mourned her way past it without entering, waiting for it to shut down and be replaced with something she'd never enter. But all through the abysmal years and the decade since then, the sandwich shop had inexplicably endured, same as she had. It was just past four, but already the end-of-day honking and traffic had begun, the ever-larger number of drivers sitting alone in their cars, pressing their horns in vain.

Stepping through the front door, Olga felt a pressure mounting in her ears, a trembling in her eyelids. She saw that the metal-rimmed counter had been replaced. The counter edge was tiled now, and behind it someone was tapping in an order on a computer screen. Two juice machines beeped and roared and Olga wondered if she had made a mistake in choosing this place.

Can I help you? a waitress behind the counter asked, and Olga shook her head, motioned for the waitress to give her a minute to sit down. Pulling herself onto the shiny new stool at the counter, she thought of all the straws Sara had chewed on here. All the flaws in Trotsky's thinking they had dissected, the Akhmatova lines they'd debated, the resentful jokes they'd made about the sexy girl who had become the lone female student with a speaking role at the Campus Commie meetings and the male leaders who'd treated her like an intermission.

And had it also been at this counter—and Olga knew it had been—that she had insisted they both go to the CC meeting the night the roundup had occurred? Sara had wanted to skip it. To sit again on one of these stools, at this same counter, and recall her insistence that afternoon caused a prickling pain in her knees. Olga readjusted her weight on the small seat but the pain needled deeper.

There's too much shouting at the meetings, Sara had said, which Olga had agreed was true but insisted they had to show up and support the movement anyway, as no one else was talking about how to address a handful of families possessing more wealth than all the rest of the island's inhabitants combined.

No one but the CC, Olga had argued, is even attempting to re-imagine this country.

But reimagining it how? Sara had asked, and brought up the CC leader at the last meeting who'd joked about admiring Hitler's ability to keep a crowd listening.

Which is why we need to show up, Olga had insisted, as if they were equally vulnerable. But it was only Sara's surname the soldiers had pronounced in a different tone at the roundup, freighting it with something more determined.

Then came the room with the boarded-over window, the soldier who kept coming in and saying Where's the Jew girl, ordering Sara to the mattress, spitting out her last name as if it were the bone of a fish he had to spit out before it choked him. When they ordered Olga and the other women from the room, Olga had pressed herself against the wall and refused to leave. But the butt of one gun and then another made it clear the choice was not hers. All she could choose was to will her mind back to the room, to the sound of Sara's hands sticking to the plastic mattress.

On the other side of the counter now, two juice machines roared monstrously to life, one sluicing apples, the other roaring up an orange pulpy blur that looked like mango. Hunched over the counter, watching the liquid splash against the sides, Olga decided she would have to hold back with this niece. At least during this first encounter, or her grief would overwhelm her as suddenly as Simon had described his stutter returning despite all his years of tactics. Olga feared even her humor would fail her if she said Sara's name here too many times.

And then, impossibly, gloriously, walking into this invincible sandwich shop was her beloved again. Unaged. Unbroken. Her hair longer and slightly darker. But with the same thick, untamable curls. The same deep-set black eyes just as sharp, just as quick to spot Olga waving and trembling, half crumbling off the stool like the ruin she was.

You're the reason, she said to the young woman before her. You're why I couldn't die.

Victor was in the bathroom when his wife intruded. He despised intrusions while he was in the bathroom and was about to remind Cristina of this, along with several other things he particularly despised about her this morning, when she shoved the just-arrived newspaper onto his bent legs.

What the hell is this? she said, her overdyed hair hanging flat around her face. What did you write this email for? How could you let something like this get leaked to the paper?

Victor spread the front page over his legs. "Leaked Email Exposes Senatorial Ties to Fecal Fiasco," the headline said, and it was by that relentless, annoying reporter with the stutter, Simon something. All the senators warned each other to avoid him.

It had to be your cousin who leaked this, Cristina said, her voice reaching its most nasal, intolerable pitch, and Victor asked her to just let him finish reading. The email quoted was one he'd sent to his cousin several years ago, assuring him that a little consultant income from a pig farm wouldn't set off any alarms, government salaries on the island being as dismal as they were. On its own, unassociated with the unprecedented lake full of shit his father-in-law's incompetent friend had produced, the message wasn't fatal. It was the context that was ruinous and he couldn't see his cousin knowing this was the quote to send. His cousin's mind wasn't attuned to what a single sentence from an old email would provoke in the media, and it occurred to Victor exactly who had to be behind this.

He flushed the toilet and moved away from it before the drops could splash the backs of his legs. He drew right up into the face of the stranger he had married, scavenging it for the truth.

It was you who went through my emails, wasn't it? he asked, his face twisting with viciousness. It was your father's idea, and you did his bidding. As you always do.

What are you talking about? Cristina drew in her bird-thin neck and he saw that she was frightened. And decided her fear was proof. He was right. She had done it.

He drew even closer and had a fleeting, furious thought of Lena's arrogance, of Maria's, as if he'd needed her sophomoric ideas when the same obvious premise for eliminating tuition had occurred to him and every sentient being in the TJP. The first time, at his place, when Maria threatened to expose him for campaigning on her ideas without giving her any credit, he'd controlled himself. He'd shouted about the Senate having no need for the juvenile calculations of some college girl. He hadn't touched her, not even once. But on the road above the Minnow, Maria had been drunker than he'd ever seen her, and angrier, accusing him of manipulating and stalking her, threatening that she had a friend who knew a reporter she was going to call if he didn't give her the credit she deserved.

In the bathroom now, he took hold of his wife's bony shoulders, his panic tearing up his stomach. You and your father forced me into this! he shouted. You made me prey on my cousin's trust and now you think you can just hurl our reputations into the garbage to save your father's?

What are you talking about? Cristina said, backing away from him.

You know what I'm talking about. He sank his thumbs into her shoulders, his capacity for restraint draining from him as swiftly as the color from his wife's face.

But then a child's high-pitched voice came from the hallway outside the master bathroom. The milk smells funny, their son called, and stillness fell over them, a grim stillness containing an honesty unlike any they'd yet allowed into their marriage.

Pack your things, his wife said, extracting herself from his grip and backing toward the door. All I have ever done is defend you, Victor. Every time you slammed the table at a meeting and shouted like a monster, it got back to me. I've defended you to every wife in the Senate, to my father, to everyone. You need to get out of this apartment. Now.

Transaction Log for Olga's
SEEK THE SUBLIME OR DIE

Ecstasy, S, that's what it was to behold your namesake.

She is brazen. In all the ways that matter, she is your spirit daughter—fierce but kind. Wary but courageous. When I asked if she was willing to collaborate with Simon, she said yes without hesitation. She bravely reported to her job today as usual. Simon and I both thought that was the safest plan for her, and she agreed. I hate thinking of her still sitting a wall away from that vengeful psychopath, but to quit right away would be too suspect, and dangerous.

The plan I had in mind, S, was for her to let me into the building somehow in the evening, for me to be the one who took the risk of being caught on his computer. But your namesake said it would be far easier for her to go through his emails herself when he was on his lunch break. I told her I couldn't put her in that position.

Yet once again, S, my role was to safely sit alone and wait. And agonize. Sara wanted to risk going on his computer on his lunch break a second time and try once more to find an email linking him even obliquely to Maria P. But Simon and I convinced her not to push her luck. I told her that, in the long human history of homicidal politicians, how many ever go to trial? The political class almost never goes down for anything but kickbacks and shit lakes.

Your namesake promised she would not risk going anywhere near his computer again and I hope she means it. She promised me and Simon she's just going to stay on, in his office, feigning loyalty for another month or two, until our stealth collaboration seeps into the underhistory of this island where the most subversive acts have always transpired.

And maybe your namesake's lone search for Maria P.'s name didn't uncover any email trace because there isn't one to find. Maybe Maria's admiring glances in Victor's direction during his speeches had nothing to do with her death. Maybe, like your intrepid namesake, when Victor repeatedly placed his hand on her back, Maria mentioned a boyfriend, or a knife in her pocket, or whatever occurred to her to fend him off.

Earnings for the Day
Emotionally, S, an all-out bonanza.

Side Business
Suspended for drastic action.

Today's Only Purpose
Free knowledge, for anyone who wants to come and get it.

I'm giving away everything in Conspiracy today, S. I can't just sit here like it's any other afternoon. This may be the only sliver from the pie of justice I'm going to get.

I put a sign out front already:

FREE FOOD
FOR THE MIND

You know there is nothing, S, that lures people up a steep road like the promise of free food. I want every book once buried in these hills to find its way back into the hands of the people who haul themselves up these damn stairwells every day. As for the eager northerners with their bulging wallets, they'll just have to browse for some other kind of book-shaped souvenir.

Freddy heard a knock outside and assumed it was at his neighbor's door. He couldn't imagine anyone bothering him this early in the morning. Off at the other end of the apartment, in the kitchen, half-asleep and still in his pajamas, he was polishing off some stale cake and considering his Socratic nature. He'd only slept a few hours, devoting most of the night to finishing his new play. It was set on an island, though not necessarily his own, and involved a generation of playwrights who all adopted Socrates as a pen name, making it impossible to identify which of them was behind any given play. He'd written biographies for all the playwrights to recite as monologues, each one full of Socrates trivia mixed in with their anonymous confessions of moral failure, dilemmas when they'd failed to heed what Socrates had called his *daimon*, or inner oracle.

At around four in the morning, Freddy had realized these anonymous confessions were the heart of the play and threw out the rest of it. He added whips for all the cast members to flagellate themselves with over their moral shortcomings, their lashings getting increasingly dramatic until they verged on sexual. After writing the last scene, closing the curtain with the entire cast still writhing on the floor, he'd felt far too frenzied to sleep. Instead, he'd scribbled another Scene to Be Incinerated.

At the long wooden counter of his kitchen, feeling as fuzzed-over as the moldy loaf of bread he'd thrown out last night, Freddy wished he hadn't switched to another scene about Victor and had just gone to bed. He could never stage a show defaming his brother, let alone one that implied Victor was a potential murderer.

From the front of his apartment, he heard the knocking again and hoped his neighbor would answer his door soon.

He shoved another forkful of stale cake into his mouth and coughed when some of the morsels stuck to the lining of his throat. He poured a glass of water, gulped it down, and felt queasy. He'd eaten almost half of the same stale cake last night during his writing frenzy. What he needed was to ingest something fresh, a piece of fruit, but he hadn't bought any. Produce had become so expensive on the island. It was outrageous, and Victor's beloved TJP, for all they carried on about marginally decreasing poverty since Cato, were doing nothing about inflation. Whether Marie Antoinette had actually said it or not, the suggestion that the poor should just subsist on cake had proved rather prescient. Cheap cake was indeed the most filling, if bloating, solution for a man with little in his wallet beyond scribbled notes and pictures of his nephew.

But oh, how he enjoyed the sight of Edgar's little earnest face tucked there into his uppermost slot. His inner daimon never posed any opposition when he decided to go on a Sunday to see his nephew. It was only after he came home that the whisper began in his mind, *Just ask him, Freddy, just step in front of your brother and ask him. Or are you too much of a coward to hear the answer?*

With a sigh, Freddy risked another bite of cake, immediately chasing it with water this time. Facing the coffee machine, he debated whether to make a pot or go back to sleep, waited for his inner daimon to weigh in, but received no guidance.

It was then, while standing in front of the empty coffee pot, his mind foggy and philosophical, that Freddy heard what sounded like someone calling his name. Someone calling it in the demanding, possessive tone Victor used with him when they were children, a tone that claimed to know him more honestly than anyone.

Freddy fixed his eyes on the cake crumbs speckling the counter as he heard the voice shout his name again, demanding he open up, followed by a banging sound that indisputably came from his kitchen window. On the other side of the dirty glass was his brother's furious face.

Open the door, Freddy! That bitch kicked me out! Victor shouted with the scowl that had become one of his increasingly permanent features. Freddy lowered his gaze once more to the dull shine of his butter knife on the counter, the hard crumbs of his breakfast.

Come on, wake up. Just open the fucking door, Victor ordered, and Freddy obeyed with the slow-footed silence of a man convinced he has no other option. He made his way to the other end of his cramped, cluttered home and granted entry to his brother.

Prostrate on Freddy's malodorous sofa, Victor listened in the dark for his brother's snores to begin. Even as a boy, Freddy had snored uproariously. Lying on the upper bunk bed, Victor had grown accustomed to the rumbling beneath him. Freddy had always been beneath him, shorter, rounder, younger, weaker. Victor was not the brother who came for help. He was the one who gave it, who'd become the most admired person in the family. Just last week, another senator had advised that as soon as he was elected to his second term he should start thinking about his campaign for president.

Uncomfortable, Victor flipped over on the couch toward the cushions but they smelled too strongly of cigarettes and mold. With disgust, he flipped back over, but that meant facing the crude cardboard cutout of Socrates that his brother had made—such an insane, pretentious thing to hang in a living room.

Victor couldn't see how he could stay here another night. This scandal couldn't last. He had Sara telling reporters that the central blame really lay with his father-in-law. He hadn't taken calls from anyone all day but Sara, who clearly believed in him more than his traitorous soon-to-be ex-wife. He'd have to give Cristina the apartment. But now he'd be able to sleep openly again with whomever he wanted. Maybe even Sara, who had rejected his advances, but she hadn't mentioned her boyfriend in weeks.

At the thought of Sara handling his calls, of his hand moving over her breasts under her shirt, Victor lowered his right hand into his boxers beneath the flimsy sheet his brother had offered him, which also smelled. He still couldn't hear any snores from the bedroom but he hadn't slept under the same roof as Freddy in, what, fifteen years? For all he knew, his brother no longer snored and had fallen right to sleep, feeling no obligation to stay up worrying about his older brother being publicly betrayed by such a vile, disloyal wife.

Victor tugged at his penis harder, causing the slack skin of his gut to quiver against the back of his hand. He'd get past this. Of course he would. He'd come out on top. At the thought, he began to sweat. No, this humiliating moment could not belong to him. He was not a man yanking off on his brother's nasty bachelor couch.

He heard a creak come from his brother's room but disregarded it. Freddy was just turning in his bed. But then he heard his brother's distinctive shuffling step and Victor flipped over to hide his erection against the cushions. I'm trying to sleep, he said to the outline of his brother in the doorway.

I want you to tell me, Freddy said.

Tell you what? Victor asked. I already told you everything that wasn't in the paper.

I'm not talking about that, Freddy said. I want to know what happened to Maria P.

SCENES TO BE INCINERATED
(WORK IN PROGRESS BY ANONYMOUS)

Empty stage, single dim light.

Front stage, in ill-fitting underwear, the senator sits in a folding chair.

Well above his head hangs a reelection sign:

REELECT A CANDIDATE OF DECISIVE
ACTION

Stage left, also in worn, unfortunate underwear, stands the senator's brother.

Both men should be unfit.

If possible, their guts should expand over their waistbands in an unsightly, middle-aged manner.

SENATOR'S BROTHER

You don't even have to answer.

Just nod.

It won't leave this room.

I'll go to bed and won't ever bring it up again.

SENATOR

There's nothing to tell you, just go to sleep.

SENATOR'S BROTHER

But were you there?

Did you maybe see her, that night?

The senator says nothing.

Above his head, the campaign sign lowers slightly.

SENATOR'S BROTHER

Okay, all right.

So you saw her on Trinity that night.

She was at the Minnow drinking with her friends.

Which is always packed with students.

Anyone who's not a student looks out of place there.

And a senator definitely can't be seen doing shots with college kids.

Or sleeping with them, right?

A pause.

So maybe you wouldn't have wanted to meet her there.

Maybe you asked her to walk up the hill to meet you?

Is that possible?

Above the senator's head, the sign lowers a little more.

SENATOR'S BROTHER

Okay, so you're waiting for her up the hill above the Minnow.

There's nothing open, right?

Just closed stores with their gates down.

And it's dark because Trinity has never had enough streetlights.

Because this port has never had enough of anything.

And maybe Maria isn't on time.

Maybe she made you wait, and you're fuming when she arrives?

Maybe she arrives a little drunk?

The campaign sign lowers further.

Beneath it, the senator remains rigid.

The lighting should be particularly shadowy here.

His face stiff and withholding.

SENATOR'S BROTHER

All right. So.

Pause.

Maria arrives.

You're fuming.

She's a little drunk.

Maybe she resents having to meet you and leave her friends.

The novelty of sleeping with a senator is wearing off.

Maybe she says this?

Maybe a tension's started over something else?

Maybe it's the reason you drove there to meet her?

The sign lowers a fraction more.

The senator might fidget here.

He might adjust his ill-fitting underwear.

SENATOR'S BROTHER

Okay, so there's been an argument before now.

Does she make a threat?

Maybe to tell everyone you're sleeping with her?

Maybe something even more damaging than that?

The campaign sign swings slightly.

A pause.

The sign continues to lower gradually through the next questions, which come faster.

SENATOR'S BROTHER

Okay, so she's threatened you.

You're panicking.

And then what?

Did you hear the bus before it reached the curve?

Because we were taught to be vigilant, right?

You can't stop listening for the fucking vans.

For someone coming up behind you.

Do you do something to Maria then, there at the curb?

The sign lowers until it conceals the senator's mouth.
It drops in front of his neck.

The lights go out.

*Two years later
in a rapidly developing valley
in the interior of the island*

Six years after the death of Maria P., Cristina was driving through the valley with her son and saw a man ahead, holding up what looked like a dead goat for sale. Produce stands were stitched along the seams of roads all over the interior. Huts selling breads or cuts of livestock were not uncommon either. But a man standing under a tree hawking a whole slaughtered animal was unusual, and Cristina found herself unable to look away from him as they drove closer. After the divorce and her decision to move with Edgar to the valley, her father had bought her a silver Land Rover, and from her elevated seat within it, the man under the tree seemed to have his eyes fixed on her as well.

She pressed her sandal down harder on the gas to speed past him, though it was really too tight a curve to accelerate. The slaughtered animal in the man's arms was large and wrapped in newspaper, its death recent enough for its blood to still be soaking through the print. The man was holding it up by its legs, which looked to Cristina, as she drove closer, a bit too shapely for the ankles of a goat. They looked almost fleshy, female.

She reached the curve, closing the distance between them. Through the windshield, she saw with horror that there were only two ankles protruding from the newspaper, not four, and they did not give way to hooves of any sort. Just above where the man was gripping the legs were the shapely feet of a woman.

Suddenly a car horn blared, and Cristina looked up to find a pickup truck coming right at her. She was in the wrong lane. In her stupor, she had stopped turning the wheel. With a gasp, she jerked the car so violently her son cried out from the backseat.

I'm so sorry. She glanced back at Edgar in the rearview mirror, then again at the man now behind them, still holding up the bloody newspaper over what had to be an animal. She willed her mind to see its hooves, nothing more than livestock intended to be sold and placed on a grill to feed a family.

But even with the gap widening between her Land Rover and the man under the tree, what hung covered in bloody newspaper in his hands still looked too hairless and human. Too shapely.

It's all right, she declared to her son. We're both fine, right? Nothing's happened. Why don't you tell me, my love, what you would like for dinner.

She pressed more firmly on the gas as the road straightened, forcing her gaze to remain on the planted fields on either side of the car, the rows of plastic tarps over the valley's legendary tomatoes. She waited for her son to respond but Edgar just stared back at her with his lips parted, his eyes wide in his small, startled face. Ahead of them, a clot of dark birds dispersed across the sky.

Each afternoon, Olga picked up her grandson and drove him home over the river known to everyone in the valley as the Maria. The boy wasn't really her grandson, and on some official map of the interior, the river most likely had another designation.

At the valley's rehab center, Olga had asked the nurses why the river was called a woman's name. But the nurses had all shrugged and said that's just what it had always been, the muddy Maria. Here and there, the slow-moving heads of horses and cows bent and sipped from it. After school, children pitched their stones into the current. In the evening, the children turned into teenagers—smoking and groping each other under the cover of the bridges, flicking their beer cans and cigarettes into the Maria.

On and on the muddy river went. Okay, Maria, here we come, Olga said now as they bumped over the planks of the bridge just after Cosmo's school, swearing under her breath at the pain radiating from her hip with each rumble of the car. She'd irrevocably shattered her left hip when she fell coming up the steps to the Sublime. She hadn't been drunk or high. She'd just slipped, stupidly, and found out in the hospital that she had severe osteoporosis. The municipal hospital near the port had botched the operation and she hadn't been able to walk properly until a surgeon related to Lena's boss at the Ministry of Education went back in and fixed things and got her into the rehab center in the valley.

In the excruciating weeks between her first surgery and the second, she recognized her days scaling the stairways of the port had come to end. To give up the Sublime had been more of a relief than she'd expected. After meeting Sara and her liberating giveaway of all the stock in Conspiracy, she'd felt an increasing desire to be unburdened of the store altogether. She'd grown weary of being trapped behind the register, being a receptacle for people's rants about literature and politics, for students' pronouncements about how much they longed for their Victor. No other politician had taken on the cause of free tuition after he lost his bid for reelection. Every afternoon, some student shuffling in for weed would indignantly insist that the media had been waiting to catch Victor at something, that the news had blown the pig farm scandal out of proportion.

None of the students seemed to take into account Victor's divorce or the power of his now ex-father-in-law. The scandal had certainly tarnished Victor's reputation, but Olga was convinced that what had really impeded him from attempting any kind of comeback yet was the end of his marriage, the likelihood of the elder senator loathing Victor enough to prevent him from running for a position with the TJP anywhere on the island.

Sometimes Olga would impart these thoughts to the students. Other days, she'd just nod during their nonstop Victor nostalgia, which had been helpful in one respect. The cult-like longing for Victor had certainly lessened her guilt about the new owners turning the Sublime into a nail salon.

After her release from the valley's rehab center, she had assumed that her stay with the newly returned Lena would last a few months, at most. Yet somehow a year had gone by as quiet and green as the fields of the valley and she was still playing grandma in the afternoons, still smoking with Lena in the evenings on the porch, watching the light sift through the trees. At breakfast, they took turns being the ornery one at the table. It was the rare morning now that Olga even considered a joint while still in bed. There was really no predicting where, or when, the least lonely years of one's adult life might begin.

Still, she knew she needed to do something more here in the valley, something on her own terms. As the road straightened past the bridge and the afternoon sunlight poured through the driver's-side window and warmed her hands, she thought again of her conversation with Lena and Sara on the porch the weekend before. They'd all been high and Olga had told them about her resentment in college of the one woman granted a speaking role in the Campus Communists meetings. Olga had intended it as an amusing anecdote, but Sara, as her namesake would have, insisted the recollection must have surfaced in her mind now for a reason.

Why don't you run for municipal council here? Sara said. Even if you don't win, you'd shake up the conversation. And who knows, there are more liberal, educated people moving out from the capital all the time. They'd vote for you, a detainee and former bookstore owner. Why not just put your name on the ballot and see what happens?

But Olga didn't want to expose herself to public scrutiny in the valley, or Lena and Cosmo to it either. They were too odd a household, too new here to risk that kind of exposure. It would be seen as arrogant for an outsider to march in with big ideas, even worse if someone managed to dig up her mother's Jewish last name. She'd invite the same sort of hostilities Cosmo had confronted at the municipal school, where a group of boys kept pushing him around at recess and calling him Tourist Face. After one boy hit him repeatedly on the head with a stick and no teacher stepped in to stop it, Lena had switched him to the only private academy in the valley considered liberal. It was where all the wealthy but left-leaning parents in the interior sent their children. Nobody had hit Cosmo yet, though the kids were just as vicious in their haughty academy way, asking why he had dots on his face and where his father was and why he had a dog's name.

How'd it go today? Olga glanced back at her small passenger in the backseat.

A little better, I guess. Cosmo shrugged, talking to the grime on the window.

Why's that?

Edgar was my partner in reading. He doesn't like anyone asking about his dad either.

Is that right? They were now passing the tomato farm they always drove by on the ride home from his new school. Over the ground, low plastic tarps extended in every direction, sheltering the tomatoes reddening beneath them. By this point in the spring, the heat in the valley was relentless enough to cast a low haze over the road and fields, giving an impression that their lives were occurring over a buried layer of steam, trapped underground.

How about we invite this Edgar over some afternoon? Olga asked. I want to meet him.

Outside the police station, Freddy sighed with self-pity. It was three a.m. and he did not want to be entering this door again. He hadn't wanted to come to the station the last time he'd been summoned here to retrieve his brother. Every corridor stank of slumped, sweaty men, other angry drunks waiting for some family member to reluctantly arrive to claim them.

A step ahead reaching the door, his boyfriend Alex held it open and assured Freddy he'd wait outside however long things took.

Freddy nodded and stepped forward alone. Neither of them knew of any gay men beaten to death since the TJP took power but that didn't mean it hadn't occurred, or that there wasn't an officer sitting in every station on the island waiting for an excuse to get away with it again.

And who else was there to claim Victor? Their mother had died. Cristina's father had covered the bail again and paid off the night officers to keep the incident out of the papers and protect his daughter and grandson. You need to pick him up now, Cristina said to Freddy when she called and woke him up. If you don't get him out of there before the next shift comes in, neither of you will ever see Edgar again.

Freddy assured Cristina he would get there as swiftly as he could. Moving from the dim, moth-filled light outside the station into the first corridor, he felt overwhelmed with gratitude for the steadying thought of Alex outside, willing to accompany him yet again on this dreadful task. The second time Alex had stayed over, Victor had shown up drunk around this same hour, shouting about what a disgusting traitor and whore he'd married, how Cristina's whole family should be in jail. Freddy had assumed Alex would feel uncomfortable and leave.

But after Victor vomited and passed out, he found Alex in the kitchen making coffee. Alex confided his mother had been a drunk and he'd made coffee with far worse going on in the living room. While Victor snored on the sofa, they'd had sex in the kitchen, after which they made another pot of coffee and swapped stories.

Perhaps it was the relentless, sputtering reminder of Victor there, a room away, or simply an openness that Alex produced in him, but by dawn, Freddy found himself telling Alex what he'd heard from Lena about Victor leaving her unconscious on the floor. And there's more, Freddy had murmured, even more brutal.

I don't know anyone on this island, Alex had replied, who isn't one degree removed from more brutality than they can bear to admit.

Two weeks later, Freddy unlocked the drawer where he stored his Scenes to Be Incinerated and passed them to Alex, then sealed himself in the bathroom until he heard the couch creak and Alex's even steps across the wooden floor. For a large-boned man, Alex moved with surprising lightness. He worked as an orderly at the municipal hospital, helping people out of beds and into the shower. Freddy had never met anyone so capable of being present without being imposing. When he emerged from the bathroom to hear Alex's reaction, he stopped in the doorway as he had the night he'd confronted Victor. I'll understand, he said, if you find me sickening for doing nothing about this.

But you did do something. Alex touched his face. You wrote it down.

Yet what had writing and locking it all in a drawer changed? This time, according to Cristina, Victor had gotten into a fight outside a bar and smashed a man's windshield with a rock. The last time, Victor had clanged some man's head against a telephone pole like the clapper of a bell. Victor had sworn the man and four others had oinked at him and pushed him outside the bar, yelling that he and his cousin should have been sold off as pork, too. But when Victor sobered up, the story changed to just one man oinking at him and Freddy realized there likely had not been any pushing at all.

Down, down the dirty corridor of the sixteenth precinct Freddy dragged himself toward the room where his brother waited, past the notice board full of pinned-up illustrations of killers and children who remained unaccounted for. At the second door, Freddy felt a dread so withering it was like the onset of a flu. But he forced himself to press the security button, to continue moving forward through another thick bulletproof door, another beep and click.

This time, he knew to brace for the sight of his brother handcuffed to the metal chair just past the warden's desk. And indeed, handcuffed to the same chair sat his once-senatorial brother with a swollen gash on his forehead and a streak of dried blood above his left eyebrow. But it was Victor's gaze that made it hardest to continue walking toward him, the terrifying indignation of their father in his brother's eyes. A voltage of rage too high for the flash of any other emotion to register in his eyes, even briefly.

Next to Victor, behind the wooden desk, the warden was balder and older than last time. He stared at Freddy with scorn. Are you the brother? he asked and Freddy nodded.

You need to state your answer. The warden dropped his hairy forearms against the desk and leaned forward. Do you think you can act like a man and answer the question? We've got rules here. I don't care if this lying bastard was a senator once or not. Are you the brother?

Freddy glanced at Victor's irate, misshapen face, and then back at the bald warden who was plainly relishing the threat in his tone, his air of violence, of viciousness. Freddy swallowed. He wondered what it would take for there to be a true reckoning with the repressive roles men imposed on each other, a moment when acting despotic would finally be recognized as the weakness that it was.

Yes, sir, he said to the warden, I am the brother.

LINEAGE IN PURGATORY
(WORK IN PROGRESS BY FMG)

SET

Four chairs.

A few paper flames pinned to the back curtain.

Harsh, hellish lighting.

Actors enter one at a time,

each dressed in a bedsheet like a Greek philosopher.

The Father enters in a worn, yellowed sheet.

He goes right to the fourth and farthest chair.

Does not acknowledge audience.

The Burdened Son emerges next, gives audience a hostile stare.

His sheet is blood-stained.

He kicks the second chair out of the row.

Sits down heavily in the third chair, beside the Father.

The Theatrical Son enters.

His sheet is wrinkled satin.

He sings an out-of-pitch aria for the audience.

*His chair is out of alignment from the kick of the
Burdened Son.*

He sits on it sideways.

Last comes a boy-size Inheritor.

*His sheet is clean and white, one end tied to something
offstage.*

*How the Inheritor's sheet is tied, offstage, should not be
visible to the audience.*

*If necessary to tie two sheets together to pull this off,
so be it.*

He yanks.

INHERITOR

I can't get to my seat.

FATHER

So what?

Do you think Purgatory makes anything easy?

THEATRICAL SON

He doesn't know, Father.

He's just come in.

FATHER

Well, he needs to be told what he's coming into.

He needs to know that all anyone's guaranteed here are time and flames.

The Theatrical Son rises, crosses to the small Inheritor.

Attempts to rip his sheet and free him.

FATHER

What the hell are you doing?

You can't tear the sheets in Purgatory.

BURDENED SON

You better stop interfering.

The Inheritor doesn't belong to you—I made him!

THEATRICAL SON

And what did you make him for?

To watch him stand here, stuck this way?

He tries to tear the Inheritor's sheet with his teeth.

FATHER

You won't be able to tear that.

Stop making a fool of yourself.

All you've ever done is make a fool of yourself.

The Theatrical Son sings another off-key aria.

He gnaws more intently on the Inheritor's sheet.

The Burdened Son rises.

BURDENED SON

You better get away from him.

You'll end up in the flames for this.

THEATRICAL SON

Or you will.

Who's the one here doing nothing to help the Inheritor?

All you care about is claiming him.

The brothers grab each other.

A few houselights flicker over the audience.

The Inheritor's sheet falls open.

Someone offstage hands him a sign:

WELCOME TO PURGATORY

The Inheritor holds the sign over his exposed parts.

Lights go down.

Lena squinted through the windshield at the low, leafy rows on either side of the road. She hoped she'd made the right turn and hadn't misunderstood the instructions on her phone. There had been no signs with the road's name. Many of the roads in the interior went unmarked for long stretches as if they had been made by, and for, whoever had grown up along them and no one else. After a year in the valley, Lena still couldn't even hazard a guess at what was hidden all around her, under the endless rows of dense leaves.

She checked the clock on her dashboard and swore. She was nearly an hour late for the school she was supposed to visit today and they dismissed at three. She had forgotten to bring anything for lunch and had yet to spot a farm stand to buy some fruit and ask if she was on the right road.

For her hunger, there was no one to blame but herself. And no one had asked her to drive out and observe the classrooms in this tiny school. She'd been the one who declared these visits were essential. She had criticized her predecessor for never bothering to observe even half the schools whose curriculum it was his job to oversee and improve.

Although at this point, given her diminishing sense of even what direction she was driving in, Lena feared she might not be observing any classrooms today either. And she was ravenous.

She rummaged in the glove compartment for a granola bar, though she knew she'd forgotten to replace her reserves there. She had thought there would come a point in her life when there would be fewer hours like this, of self-recrimination so wrenching and overwhelming it felt as if she were devouring herself, wordlessly slicing up her soul just to stuff it back in her own mouth.

She hadn't realized her decision to visit every school in the valley would require this many hours lost on roads with no signs, and no one out tending to whatever was growing along them. She'd have to buy something to eat from the vending machine once she found the school—if it had a working vending machine. A school she visited the month before had not even had a working water fountain. In the classroom she'd observed there, two windows had been patched with masking tape and cardboard. Halfway through the class, a scrawny, feral-looking cat had slipped beneath the cardboard and hissed at a boy seated near the window. The teacher remarked on none of it. He'd just gone on lecturing in a resigned monotone until the cat drew closer and the boy smacked it with a notebook.

It's happened before, the teacher told Lena after the class ended, and she promised him she would rally on his behalf for a replacement window, though from the way the man nodded, she knew he didn't expect it to happen, and despite her repeated calls for emergency funding, nothing had been done yet. The TJP budgeted little more for municipal schools than what they'd received under Cato. And no one, since Victor, had given more than lip service to the increasingly prohibitive cost of the college entrance exam, and of the universities themselves. In the capital, a leaderless, mostly online movement had begun to launch a Green Party. But there was also a newly formed, far better organized and funded conservative coalition called the United Front that had begun to gain seats by running ads about cracking down on the recent epidemic of carjackings and armed robberies.

When Lena made the trip out to the coast with Cosmo to see her family, she tried to dissuade her father and brothers from voting for the Front, insisting the same fascists who worked for Cato were behind it. But her brothers shrugged at this and said the TJP was doing nothing for businesses but taxing them. Lena was grateful they could at least disagree with each other aloud now, though it only increased her humiliation when she accepted her father's check for Cosmo's tuition. She abhorred the capitulation these transactions represented, the smug satisfaction with which her family responded at the news she was taking Cosmo out of the municipal system after less than a year. All her colleagues at the Ministry sent their kids to academy schools in the valley. They urged her to get over her feelings of hypocrisy, insisting Cosmo's well-being had to come first.

She liked to fantasize that if she'd gotten pregnant with the child of anyone but a tourist as pale and blond as Oscar, she would have found a way to keep him in the municipal system. She had not expected motherhood to water her down this relentlessly, to dissolve her into the muck of compromise over and over.

And why were there still no signs anywhere on a road this long? How was a person to have any sense of where she was?

Exasperated, Lena pulled over onto the strip of dirt along the interminable rows of leaves and called Olga. I can't find the school, she said. I was supposed to be there an hour ago. And I'm really hungry.

So come home and go another day, Olga said. I've got two elves here making dinner. Cosmo brought his new friend home with us, who's very serious. But we're going to loosen him up, aren't we, elves?

Lena heard in Olga's voice that she was high, very high, and hoped the boy's mother wouldn't notice when she came for her child. After they hung up, Lena could not bring herself to start the car just yet. A faint half-moon floated over the field on the left. On both sides rang a silence as crisp as a bell.

As she occasionally did when alone and flustered, she pulled up Oscar's email address on her phone, pressed it with her finger to make it appear in a new message box, then canceled the message only to repeat the sequence—fingertip hovering above his address, pressing it again.

Nothing but clouds.
From the ground, Victor couldn't make out much else.
He hadn't intended to come up Trinity Hill.
Not that evening. Not this one either.
He didn't even like the bars on this hill.
Half of them packed with children pretending to know things.
The rest with men like his father drinking themselves into children.
Nah, that can't be him, he heard a man say.
I remember seeing him in the paper all the time, another said.
Clouds.
Clouds.
Clouds.
Victor turned his heavy head to the turning ground.

It's just a rumor, Cristina said to her aunt as she drove toward her son's school. I know the girl introduced Victor at a few marches, but he wasn't involved with her. When politicians fall out of favor, people spread all sorts of nasty rumors that aren't true. But I really have to go, she said, I'm outside Edgar's school.

Cristina was still another ten minutes away, but she had conveyed what was necessary. She hadn't let another call go unanswered. That first night with Victor at the Zodiac, she hadn't grasped what Maria the shrill woman in the lobby had been shouting about. She'd been too distracted by the bull-like way the woman had charged at them from across the lobby. Victor had obviously slept with her at some point, as Cristina assumed he had with the woman who'd inquired about Victor's connection to Maria P. at a dinner party the week before their wedding. The second woman had seemed just as bull-like and resentful. Cristina had dismissed both of them as jealous, bitter that Victor had chosen to marry her instead. She had felt so triumphant during those months before the wedding, walking into parties with her hand tucked under the arm of the handsome senator most likely to be the next presidential candidate for the TJP. Her father had assured her that Victor wouldn't be able to run for any public office again. But the worst possible rumors kept on surfacing anyway.

Crossing the last bridge now before Edgar's school, she glanced down at the muddy rush of the Maria below. It was the third call this week she had received inquiring about Victor and the pretty girl who'd introduced him at the marches, the one who died on Trinity Hill. If she didn't keep answering at least some of the calls, Cristina knew she would end up feeding the rumor, engorging it into the monstrosity it was bound to become regardless.

With dread, she looked down at the large, harsh rocks jutting up through the river. If this narrow bridge gave way and pitched her car into the Maria, she wondered which would end her first, one of those rocks, or the muddy water.

Oscar closed the door to his daughter's room and crept toward the living room thinking of the tigers they'd seen the previous weekend at the zoo, the irrelevance of their stealth, moving toward nothing but the bars at the opposite end of their single-tree, seven-rock savannah. He always felt far freer in his first seconds creeping toward the sofa than he did when he reached it just to sprawl there, reading headlines on his phone like some animal slumbering with its eyes open.

Over in the kitchen, he saw that his daughter had smeared avocado on the tray of her booster seat. If he didn't clean it soon, it was going to harden. But this thought did not compel him from the sofa. His wife would be home in an hour. He could clean the seat then.

As for the cracker crumbs he could feel underneath him on the sofa, he just went on tapping his screen. A notification popped up that he had a new message on Facebook. He tapped into Messenger, guessing someone from his stay-at-home-dads group was around for a playdate tomorrow after all.

When he saw the name Lena, he thought it must be a coincidence. Except there was the thumbnail image of her chiseled face, that keen stare in her dark eyes, her alluring mouth. And she had sent an attachment. He scrolled down and saw it was a photo. A boy who looked so much like him that Oscar felt a rushing movement in his mind as if he were in a swing cut from its cable midair. Had he given Lena a childhood photo of himself?

But he knew he had not. And the boy was wearing a T-shirt with a logo in the language of the island.

Hi, Oscar, the message began. *I tried to reach you at the email address you gave me at Freddy's show but I must have written it down incorrectly. Or maybe your email has changed since then. With your wife expecting, it didn't seem like the moment in your life to tell you about Cosmo. He is six now. . . .*

Oscar scrolled down to the photograph, flicked back up to the words, waiting for the frantic movement of his finger to diminish his sense of vertigo. In the rest of the message, Lena emphasized three times that she was not contacting him for financial reasons. She assured him that her family was well-off and supportive, that the only reason she was writing was just to open a line of communication for the future, in case Cosmo at some point expressed a strong desire to find the father who had given him what the kids at school called "his tourist face."

Tourist face. Oscar gaped again at the photo. The small stranger with his upturned ski-jump nose and freckles. The same thick, blond hair, which Lena had let grow as long as his own. It flopped over the boy's small forehead. Oscar hadn't realized how long he'd sat there staring at the photo until he heard his daughter cry out from her room, her cry as familiar to him as his own voice.

How could he be both of these men? The father able to pick out his daughter's cry in a crowd of twenty children, and the one responsible for this little stranger with his face? Parenthood was the one dimension of his life about which he felt no inadequacy or ambivalence. About which he felt imminently capable and proud. Every day, he woke up aching to hold his kid again, to be her father.

He tried to expand the image of Cosmo with his fingertips but the Messenger box wouldn't allow him to enlarge it. In her toddler bed, waiting for him to appear, his daughter was wailing, her cries escalating into primal howls. He was just about to get up and go for her when the door slammed open, giving way to the flushed face of his wife. My God, Oscar, what happened? I could hear her screaming from the stairwell. What are you doing, just sitting there on the couch?

Even then, he could not will himself to put down the phone.

Lena pulled up to the gated entrance and checked to see if anyone she knew was driving by. She didn't want to be observed picking up her son here, at this hideous development, with its plastic-sided houses and groomed lawns that looked straight out of some northerner horror film. When people complained about wealthy newcomers ruining the area, they always brought up the blemish of this new gated development, how profoundly at odds it was with the farmland and produce stands, with the old barns and silos and everything along the road before this sudden cluster of ugly, soulless homes.

As she waited for the guard to open the gate, Lena spotted Cosmo's blond head in one of the first driveways, riding with his friend in a little motorized red car. Lena had asked Olga to find out more about Edgar's mother but Olga didn't like to interact much with the parents in the academy. Lena felt guilty for knowing so little about who this new friend was seated beside her son in such an enormous, beeping, bourgeois monstrosity of a toy.

She hoped Cosmo would move on to another friend soon who lived somewhere else, then felt immediately ashamed at the thought. What kind of a mother indulged in such a desire at the sight of her son enjoying himself after school with another child? Even if that child's name was one she still associated with Victor's uncle and the boyhood picture of him she'd passed every time she entered their home. In one of their all-night sessions in the basement, Victor had told her about a night he found his father on the floor in front of the picture, weeping. Uncertain what other response beyond her body Victor would welcome, Lena had drawn closer and kissed him, had said nothing when he roughly placed her beneath him on the floor, though the floor was painful under her tailbone, and cold.

Stepping out of her car, she forced a smile at Edgar's mother stepping out of the house onto the porch. She'd been intrigued when Olga told her Edgar apparently didn't live with a father either. Lena had imagined a possible friendship. But not with a mother who would choose to live in such a heinous development.

No, she couldn't possibly have any connection with a mother like this.

Cristina swatted at the mosquitoes as she made her way down the driveway to meet Cosmo's mother. At dusk, she didn't linger outside if she could avoid it. She wished someone had warned her about the mosquitoes in the interior. With no breeze from the ocean, the mosquitoes feasted from long before sunset until well after dark. She found it primitive, having to factor in the mouths of insects for so many hours every evening. She required the gardener to mow their lawn weekly and apply insecticide, and at least they had less of a problem than most people in the valley.

When she'd picked up Edgar at his friend's the other night, she'd been shocked at how overgrown and weedy the mother had permitted the property to become, the number of mosquitoes clouding the yard. Cristina had made up an excuse to hustle Edgar straight to the car. She'd been surprised at what an oddly isolated old house Cosmo's mother had chosen, off a dirt road and with cracked tiles on the roof. The babysitter, Olga, had been odd as well, coming to the door with her sweater misbuttoned and her gray hair cut close to the scalp like a man's. She had looked old enough to be Cosmo's grandmother, but spoke with as much slang as someone in college, or younger.

Olga had seemed intelligent, however, and joyful. Edgar had come skipping out of the house, the most relaxed she'd seen him since she'd kicked Victor out. The sight of her son hooking his arm around a boy with such a freckled, stereotypical northerner face had unnerved her, though Cristina knew she was in a poor position to judge a child based on any assumptions about his father. She was in no position at all, in fact. She was desolate with loneliness, had been restless all day, hoping she'd find a way to hit it off with this mother, maybe invite them over together the next weekend.

Although she hoped the mother wouldn't insist on reciprocating, or not until the weather cooled a bit and the mosquitoes thinned.

As Lena emerged from her car, the boys came beeping down the street again, and Cristina mimed a wheel between her hands as she made her way down the driveway, willing her mouth into a broad smile.

They've had such a good time in that car, Cristina called to Lena and waited for her to agree. But Lena just stared back at her from the curb with what looked like alarm, a notable tension in her mouth. Cristina had a feeling they had met before but couldn't recall where. In the car, Cosmo had told her that his mother worked for the Ministry of Education, but Cristina couldn't imagine a person in a very high position living in such a dilapidated house. And Lena had arrived in the sort of baggy, flowered tunic sold at street fairs, the fabric cheap-looking, unflattering.

I've kept watch for any cars, Cristina assured her, and with the gate, they're really quite safe riding down the street here.

You're Victor's wife, Lena said.

Cristina felt the sting of a mosquito on her cheek but didn't lift her hand. Ex, she said, and watched Lena step backward. Cosmo called from the street, asking his mother to watch how fast they could go. The boys made a U-turn and just missed the curb, but Lena looked toward them for only a moment before whipping back around, her eyes agitated, almost frantic.

Did Victor take a job out here? she asked. Does he come to their school?

Never. Cristina shook her head and explained that Victor was working for a shipping company in the port. We make arrangements for all the visits there, she added, at his brother's.

Good old Freddy, right? Lena crossed her arms and Cristina teetered back a step as Lena continued, insisting she knew how often Victor wielded his brother's goodwill to his own benefit.

Please. They're coming back. Cristina gestured to where the boys were already swerving toward the driveway, laughing and beeping in the irritating car her parents had bought. She felt obligated to keep every gift they gave her, after all she'd asked from them to help her flee here to the interior and start again. She had exhausted herself filling out a thousand extra forms in order to register Edgar at the school under her mother's last name to avoid gossip among the parents. She thought she had cleared a path for him here, for both of them.

For Edgar's sake, she said, I'd appreciate it if you didn't share any . . . any thoughts about Victor with anyone at school.

Any thoughts about Victor, Lena repeated with a wry laugh, flicking at a mosquito in front of her face. You mean about Maria P., those thoughts? Maybe you don't remember. We met at the Zodiac.

Cristina tilted forward, felt a sharp pebble under her shoe.

Yes, I do recall, she said in her most officious tone, but I can assure you that I don't have any more information now than when you asked me then. I'm aware of the rumors, she said, lowering her voice on the "u" as if speaking of some unsightly mildew. But we all know politicians are subject to hearsay. I grew up around some of the most influential figures in the TJP, and I promise you, there is no one who is spared.

The longer Cristina continued in this tone, the more possible it became to fully inhabit the stiff posture she'd long assumed in photographs beside her father. She went on to declare her foremost responsibility for Edgar, to speak as little as possible about the past for his sake, and hoped that Lena, as a mother herself, would understand how—

Of course, I understand! Lena interrupted, her voice slipping into an impatient, clipped intonation that gave her away, Cristina recognized, as having likely gone to one of the conservative academies north of the port. The academies where the wealthiest supporters of Cato sent their children. Surprised at this, she looked over Lena's cheap bohemian tunic and leggings again with new eyes.

Perhaps you know, Cristina said, how impossible it can be to start over on this island.

Olga took her time crossing the gravel outside the town hall. She took her time opening the heavy wooden door. All she planned to do was ask a few questions. She'd left the house with the intention of going to the grocery store. With Cosmo off to Edgar's after school, she'd needed another reason to get out of the house. Partway to the store, the sight of the town hall coming up on the left had beckoned to her like a bakery. She was just going to ask out of curiosity, just to find out exactly how complicated it might be to add a name to the council ballot.

Already she was savoring the pleasure of recounting this spontaneous stop to Lena and Sara, enjoying their surprise that she had pulled in here and taken this idea a little bit further. After Sara brought up the idea on the front porch, Olga had not been able to resist considering what her name might look like on a ballot line—what a consolation it would be to witness that little green box next to the O of her name. She'd given up her Sublime, had accepted that the amnesty laws weren't going to be repealed in her lifetime, or not before all the monsters who worked for Cato had died without a single one of them going on trial.

Two cement steps led up to the door of the town hall and Olga winced as she hauled her bad hip up the first step and then the other. The front corridor was narrow, empty except for a giant photocopier with a dusty OUT OF ORDER sign taped to its lid. Above the copier hung a row of equally dusty horseshoes. Olga had expected to feel intimidated, but who could be intimidated by a hallway with nothing but a broken printer and a bunch of horseshoes?

Simon had recently written a scandalous report on mayors all over the island who'd been active in the formation of Truth and Justice who now brazenly doled out jobs to unqualified family members and wrote off their vacations as business trips. The mayor of their district in the valley hadn't been named in the piece, but from the state of the copier and the absolute quiet, it didn't look like the mayor or any municipal employees were spending much time in the building.

At the thought of all the unqualified relatives who might be on the district payroll sitting at home watching movies, Olga picked up her pace toward the only open door in the corridor. The council positions were unpaid and supposed to be filled by concerned citizens of the district, which she was.

She peeked her head into the open doorway and found a young man with a goatee inside, sitting behind an old wooden desk. He was packing handfuls of potato chips into his mouth without moving his eyes from his computer screen. He looked like he could be a nephew of the mayor. Or maybe an aimless grandson. With each handful of chips delivered into his open mouth, a cascade of crumbs fell and clung to his goatee. Hobbling closer to his desk, Olga felt a twist of nostalgia for the Sublime, for all the curious behavior she'd gotten to observe there, sleepy-faced young men like this one stumbling in for weed, as unaware of the chips in their facial hair as they were of the potential addictive pleasure of Kundera, or the sensual existentialism of Duras.

Hello, she said.

Hello, the young man replied, smashing more chips into his mouth.

Might you have any information about the municipal council election and who's running this year?

Same bunch as always, I think. He yawned. Here's the list. He held out a sheet to Olga and she asked him about the single female name, at the bottom.

Her? Oh, her husband died and she started coming to the meetings instead.

Is she the only one? Olga asked.

Only what? The young man crumpled his now empty bag of chips and tossed it in the trash can beside his desk.

The only woman on the council?

He shrugged, eyeing Olga a bit sideways, as most men in the valley did when they spoke to her, as if her close-cut hair made them uneasy, or the width of her shoulders, her unusual height for a woman on the island.

As she had gotten used to doing, she pretended this sideway staring was not happening and asked him what the process was to get a name added to the ballot.

With a tug at his goatee, he told her there was probably a form for that somewhere in the building. But he didn't pick up the phone on his desk. He didn't open a drawer. Waiting in front of him, Olga ran her tongue over the back of her teeth. The Akhmatova poems she'd been reading that morning crackled inside her like kindling. *As if they brutally knocked her flat.* But also, from "Elegy for N.N.": . . . *the heart which does not die when one thinks it should.*

Is there someone in the building, she asked, who would know where the form might be?

On the opposite side of the desk, the young man shrugged again. He wiped some bits of chips off the edge of the desk and then wiped that same hand over his mouth. Watching him, it occurred to Olga there was really nothing this island could possibly kill in her that it hadn't killed in her already. If people in the valley were offended by the sight of some newcomer on the ballot, then they would be offended. If they found out her mother's religion and didn't like it, so what? She wasn't going to win regardless. She could just add her name as a symbolic civic act of provocation, to spark a few questions with the mere sight of an Olga on the ballot, some woman with the nerve to think she might have an idea or two worth sharing with her district.

If she had to explain her motivation, she could stick to things people here would be most willing to hear from a retired bookseller— the lack of a single library in the entire valley, the problem of people dumping their bottles and other garbage at night in the Maria. She could try and keep it benign enough to avoid creating any potential turmoil for Cosmo or Lena. She could avoid bringing up the abysmal state of the municipal schools.

On the other side of the desk, the young man yawned again. I can ask about the form, he said, but the candidate will have to fill it out.

That's no problem, Olga told him. I'm the candidate.

Dear S, reporting to you from the gravel lot of the tiniest of town halls in the interior. My need to speak to you was so great I am resorting to a page from Cosmo's cookie-shaped notebook in the backseat. I added an Olga to the list of candidates for you, S, and I want you to know I am, and will always remain, your widow. Even if there is no chance of my being widowed into this two-bit council of old men, or into any entity at all in this fascist-hearted country of ours.

To put oneself out there just to lose, and publicly, should not make a widow giddy, S, but I am. I haven't smoked since lunch but am chuckling over this cookie-shaped missive to you anyway. I just am.

Victor swigged to cut the wet bite of the night wind on his face.
No one was supposed to be on the docks at this hour.
But he was keeping to the vast shadows of the largest ships.
They were all foreign, these beasts with the widest, deepest shadows.
Somebody on this island had to piss on their locked entry gates.
Swig swig.
It was Victor.
He pissed on the gate of a foreign ship.
Then he slipped on his own drips.
Or it was the slick dock that brought him down.
The uncaring ocean that was to blame.
Or his own urine on the planks.
Difficult to know when lying on a wet dock at this dim an hour.
Victor tried to resituate his legs, made it as far as his side.
The fall had been harder than he expected.
Eyes shut, he told himself he'd still run for mayor next year.
He'd run for the Green Party.
He couldn't let his ex-wife's father determine his life.
He'd rise again to where he belonged.
People loved a good resurrection.

Oscar made an endive salad to please his wife. He poached a wild salmon for her and lit the verbena candle she liked. He sprinkled rosemary over the heirloom potatoes he had slow-roasted in the oven while preparing himself for his declaration. The day the photo of Cosmo arrived, he'd shared it with his wife. When she insisted that they keep what she called "this situation" between them, and tell no one, not even his parents, he had agreed. His wife had dictated the response she wanted him to send to Lena and he had sent it:

This is a tremendous shock, Lena. I need to discuss this matter with my wife. We'll respond next week.

For the next week, he had kept his discomfort with this initial response to himself, had quietly endured his wife's furious expressions across the table over the head of their daughter. In bed together, he had accepted her careful avoidance of eye or bodily contact as if he were a suspect stranger in the adjacent seat of an airplane. When his wife asked repeatedly if he realized what a horrible, impossible situation he had created for them and for their daughter, he told her the enormity of it never left him.

That morning, as his wife stuffed her keys and water bottle into her public radio tote bag, she had looked across the kitchen counter at where he was washing their breakfast dishes and said she had a feeling this woman was going to start demanding money. There must be a reason, his wife had insisted, why this Lena never mentioned to you what her family did. It must be something shady. Have you ever seen any article about that island that didn't mention corruption? Did you look up that link I sent you about the savage robberies there, the carjackings? It's a brutal place, Oscar. This woman might resort to physical threats to our family. You don't know anything about her.

To all of this, Oscar had penitently lowered his head and scrubbed harder at the inner walls of his daughter's plastic sippy cup. The cup was dishwasher safe but he and his wife agreed it was better to wash it by hand, given the risk of extreme heat in the dishwasher causing chemicals in the cup to leach into their daughter's water. When it came to plastics and children, they fervently agreed a parent could never be careful enough.

It wasn't until his wife left for work and he'd collapsed on the rug next to his daughter and her wooden animal figurines that he began to feel increasingly numb, the truth flowing through him like anesthetic, cutting off his ability to feel the figurines between his fingers, his tongue dull and heavy in his mouth. For the truth was he could not have a child he did not know. He would die inside if he didn't return to the island to meet his son.

And so the endive tonight. The wild salmon and overpriced heirloom potatoes. He had decided the best way to convey this truth to his wife would be bluntly. But only after they'd tucked in their daughter and he'd served the salmon. Only after his wife had recounted in detail her third meeting with the potential new donor for the arts center where she oversaw fund-raising.

I need to meet him, Oscar said as his wife punctured a potato with her fork.

Meet who? She drove her fork in deeper, her blond hair falling over her forehead.

You know who I mean, he said. Cosmo. They call him Tourist Face. He has no father and he doesn't look like anyone around him.

Oh Jesus, Oscar. Don't you dare try and cast yourself as the noble savior in this. Don't even try. His wife shoved her plate hard enough to send her fork clanging to the floor. It's just so enraging. She crossed her arms. I mean, to force a connection now—

Force a connection? He's my son! How can you not understand this, as a mother? He gripped the edge of the table and saw the skin around his wife's mouth quiver for a second before she shot up from her chair. Without a word, she bolted from the table toward the long windows at the end of their living room.

I'm sorry. I shouldn't have said that. Oscar rose and started across the carpet but his wife warned him not to come any closer. In the middle of their nubby wool living-room rug, he stopped and stared at her bony back through the thin fabric of her gray wrap dress, her clenched hands at her sides. She had come to a halt so close to the window she was nearly touching the glass with her nose.

You already wrote to her about this, didn't you? his wife asked.

Yes, he said, feeling all that had been solid between them beginning to liquefy, the edges of their marriage melting as if it had consisted of no more than a block of ice.

This child exists, and he's mine, he said, and waited for his wife to reply. Beyond her, the city glittered to itself, glowing in every direction from the lit windows in the new high-rise across the street and in the even larger high-rise next to that in their ever denser, more gentrified neighborhood, which they agreed had lost its spirit but also concurred it would be foolish to leave, with the new playground opening just down the block.

I'm sorry to complicate our family this way. He ventured a step closer. But I need to at least meet him online. For now, he added, and felt the drip, drip between them quickening.

Lena set down her laptop amid the Legos on the red play table. She flipped up the screen and angled it to minimize the glare from the lamp. After Oscar's business-like first message, his second message asking to meet Cosmo over Skype had surprised her. Lena wished she knew what kind of negotiating had occurred with his wife between the messages.

Cosmo had said yes right away to the idea, but it had been a child's yes, with no knowledge of how certain fraught decisions could operate in one's life like a virus, spreading through the nervous system—how profoundly this choice might change how he saw himself and spoke, how much he might come to mistrust his own instincts.

Okay, you ready? she asked. You don't have to do this.

I'm fine, just click on it! Cosmo urged her. See if he's there.

Lena typed in her password, clicked, and saw Oscar was already logged in. With another click, Oscar's pale, freckled face filled the screen. He was grinning, but it was a forced smile, fragile and anxious. Jowl lines had deepened around his mouth and his hairline had receded. A network of lines now surrounded his eyes. Wow, Cosmo, look at you, Oscar said with his heavy accent, though Lena had assured him Cosmo spoke easily in both languages after his two years in northerner preschools.

Is that your room? Oscar leaned forward, his upturned nose magnified as if he were about to emerge from the screen, and it struck Lena how differently his pale, freckled face registered to her now that it also belonged to her son. To categorically feel a remove from such a face was no longer possible.

You have the same dots on your nose, Cosmo said, and Lena began her retreat, to give them space. As she backed out of view, she saw a flicker of Oscar's wife behind him in a green dress, retreating at the same instant. A pained laugh rose in Lena's throat but she forced herself to swallow it. Of all the women to find herself moving in fleeting synchronicity with—Oscar's smug wife, whose patronizing comments Lena had replayed often in her mind, using them to recharge her sense of righteousness and purpose.

Really? You have a book of poetry you bought from Olga? Cosmo asked, and after a nod, Oscar ducked and reappeared on the screen holding up the yellowed anthology. Half the cover was torn off, the pages uneven from all the corners he'd folded over. Lena, moved at the sight of the book, and at Oscar's thoughtfulness to plan this display of connection, drew closer.

It has one of my favorite poems in it, he said.

About growing old without finding the holy city, Lena said. I remember.

After lowering the screen, Oscar rose from the edge of the bed where he had been sitting during the call. He placed his hands on his wife's shoulders, careful not to rest too much of his weight there, and thanked her. I thought that would be harder, he said and waited for his wife to agree. But she didn't. She didn't pull away either and he thought of all the drifting he had done to get away from his warring parents, all the dropping out and starting again to avoid living with a tension that felt irresolvable, but the irresolvable had found him anyway in the form of a little boy with his face.

You're going to be thinking about this child now, his wife said, when you're with our child.

Nothing will change for our family, he assured her. I won't allow anything to change—I promise. Although already a room had formed in his mind with Cosmo in it, kneeling in front of the red Lego table where the laptop had been resting, positioning the little plastic trees around his half-finished mobile home set, waiting for his father to call again.

They brainstormed for the campaign until after midnight. Fueled on popcorn and supermarket wine, they sat out on the porch until they decided "a new advocate" had the right ring to it. People like the word "new," Sara said from the broken porch swing. It makes them think of shiny new cars and appliances, but it still acknowledges you're an outsider.

Here comes my new appliance. Olga moved in front of the porch table and stuck out her broad backside in her gray sweatpants. How's that shine?

I need my sunglasses. Lena covered her face. The shine is blinding me.

I think we've got it. Sara held up a piece of Cosmo's construction paper with the slogan scribbled across it: A New Advocate for Literacy in District 26. Who could resist the shine of that?

I'm b-b-blinking all the way out here, Simon called from where he was peeing against one of the trees by the driveway. He'd driven out with Sara for what they'd named in the car Operation Olga for the Universe.

Olga rolled back her shoulders to ham it up for them a little more. She'd pulled something in her left shoulder last week and rolling it sent a pain pulsing up into her neck. She hadn't wanted to go all out this way, with an official slogan and radio requests. All she'd wanted was to put down her name after the other widow. But Sara and Simon had insisted that if she was going to run, she had to show she meant it, and she had admitted they were right. If she didn't take this seriously, she would make it that much easier to dismiss any other woman brave enough to add her name. But she couldn't see herself getting on the radio and making any of the stilted statements Sara had come up with, referring to herself as a small-business owner, or a literacy advocate.

I'm going to get this out to FM 90 first thing tomorrow, Sara said, tapping away on her laptop, and somewhere we need to work in Lena's statistic about schools getting more money for soccer equipment than library books. It's so outrageous. Sara shook her head exactly as her namesake had done and Olga savored the ache of it. They were making far too much effort for a campaign that would go nowhere. But for this evening alone, brainstorming in the dark with her favorite living beings, the awkward disappointment to come—when nobody but a few parents from Cosmo's class voted for her—she could bear it.

And you have to b-b-bring up the Harvest Chemicals report, Simon urged. You have to read at least some of the list on the air.

If I even get on the air, Olga said. Simon had sent her a report a few days ago listing all the toxins in the runoff from Harvest Chemicals being discharged into the valley's groundwater. But Simon had also mentioned a journalist in the capital who'd written about the report. The day his story ran, the journalist came out of his apartment building and found his front tires slashed.

All day, anticipating this gathering, Olga's thoughts had clacked like the keys of a typewriter. The rhythm of the clacking had only gotten faster as the hour of Sara and Simon's arrival approached. At breakfast, she'd asked if Lena was okay with the possible backlash that reading the toxin report on the radio might create. It's possible, Olga had added, that no more than a handful of old people in their cars will be listening anyway. But it only takes one old crazy bastard to find our address and break a window.

Well, I ordered windows for this house once already, Lena had replied as they sipped their coffee. They're all standard-size. They only took a week to arrive.

On the veranda now, from under the lopsided porch swing, Lena was extracting a bag of what looked like lumps of cotton balls soaked in various colors of paint, blue and green and bright yellow.

What the h-h-hell are those? Simon asked.

Rainbow beards for the campaign, Lena said, only for covert use, of course. For our morale, here on the porch.

You're something else, Olga snorted, and before selecting a beard, she bent for the last of the burnt kernels in the popcorn bowl. Living together, she and Lena had discovered they both liked to bite down on the hard, resistant kernels at the bottom of the bowl, to brace for the one that might break their teeth.

On the runway in the capital, Freddy clicked his seat belt and slipped a piece of gum to Alex beside him before unwrapping his own. He relished their daily gestures to each other, the intimacy of them. Belonging to someone other than his brother had been like flicking the lid off an airless box he had not realized he'd been hiding in. He was not a fan of spearmint gum, but he'd gotten Alex's favorite spearmint brand for them to chew during takeoff. Symbolic acts of selflessness came so easily to Alex. Freddy found he had to make a more deliberate effort and hoped the reason was simply his unfamiliarity with the art of such gestures. His parents had never indulged each other's preferences without resentment. With Alex, it had become plainer to him how little grace there had been in his childhood when it came to kindness.

And in no segment of his life had there ever been a moment like this, sitting beside someone he loved on a red-eye to Paris. Beyond the illuminated tarmac of the runway, only a few lights from the capital showed through the darkness. Every time he left the country, Freddy had an intimation of the island's edges drawing closer, its size diminishing with each flight he took away from it. A small French company was producing *Where He Danced While We Lay Dreaming*. Freddy had tried to encourage the company to produce *Even You Are Socrates Now* instead. He was so tired of going abroad and endlessly rehashing the Cato years for strangers to sigh over. But it was the only play foreign directors wanted. It was what had gotten him and Alex on this flight to Paris, the first for both of them.

On his lap, Freddy's phone began to vibrate, the screen pulsing with his brother's name. He had never assigned an image to Victor's number. All that pulsed when his brother called was the name. Victor. Victor.

Victor.

Victor.

Victor.

Maybe something's happened, Alex said beside him.

Maybe. Freddy chewed faster, the spearmint reaching its peak sharpness, tingling his tongue.

The phone pulsed again and he felt excruciatingly aware of Alex beside him witnessing his inaction, the rising number of calls from Victor he could not bear to answer.

I thought we would've taken off by now. Freddy chewed even faster, looking toward the front of the plane to see if the stewardesses were seated yet, but they were still circulating. The phone vibrated another time and he thought of the police station, the pulpy gash on his brother's forehead, his father's terrifying rage on Victor's face.

Departure music, Alex said, passing one of the earbuds from his phone for them to listen together. Freddy pushed the bud into his ear and sank into the exquisitely unpredictable chords of Claude Debussy. The performance of some yearning person who'd gradually mastered the notes of *Rêverie*. Louder, please, he murmured to Alex as his phone pulsed again against his leg.

Victor extracted his flask and found it empty.

But how could that be, when the sound of his steps was still so firm?

Thump. Thump.

Thump.

Or no, those were not his steps, were they, and now he saw whose.

Another man in the gulping shadows of the foreign ships.

In the faint mist moving up through the planks.

Some dockworker, hands jammed in his pockets, drawing closer.

An awful peppery odor on the man's breath.

An odd smell, and Victor couldn't make out the man's face either.

Mind ablur, he heard the man murmur what sounded like sinister.

Or was it sister.

He heard I know you and did it.

The words spit out like the man had something hidden in his mouth.

Hold on, I don't want to wake Edgar, Cristina whispered to her father, hurrying in her nightgown down the staircase to the living room. Yet on the edge of the last step, she found she could not descend any further, could do nothing but grip the railing as her father described the video. A foreign dockworker who'd been in the country for only a few days who'd been choked and dragged unconscious to the end of the dock.

It's definitely Victor. I watched it several times, her father said before describing a second video his contact in the police force had sent to him as well, taken from the same shipping company's security camera a few nights before. Her ex-husband drunk and urinating all over the gate of the same foreign ship. The dockworker, they presumed, had come out to ask Victor not to urinate on their gate again.

They're going to make both videos public, her father said. There's nothing I can do about something this horrific, Cristina, and you shouldn't see it. Victor just . . . chokes the life out of the man. There's no pleading self-defense. You and Edgar should really leave the island by early tomorrow.

Leave for where? she asked, her throat closing, her tongue feeling thick and strange as she noticed someone out on the road in front of her house.

It doesn't matter where. I'll arrange something. Just get your things together and be ready to go straight to the airport in the morning. Why you married this monster is beyond me.

And without a word of reassurance, her father was gone. She was alone descending the last step to the bottom of her stairs. Outside, the figure appeared to have drawn closer. Cristina had not been able to find any curtains that felt right for their new life here in the valley and so there was nothing to pull shut now, no curtain to stop her from registering the tall, long-haired woman just past the curb, the woman's sudden jerking movement as if struck from behind.

Cristina closed her eyes to make the figure vanish. But when she opened her eyes the woman was still there, illogically upright after being struck that hard, a silhouette in the dim glow of the streetlight, the dewy tips of the grass blades glistening in the lawn in front of her.

You no longer exist, she said at once to the silhouette at the edge of her lawn and to her own faint reflection in the glass.

Freddy entered the café for his interview with *Le Monde* half an hour early. He wanted to be well into a cappuccino he'd bought himself when the journalist arrived. He felt more in control when he played against the expectation of the impoverished playwright from the island nation grateful for a free drink. He could buy his own damn latte, and he liked arriving early enough to pick the table and skim through a few emails on his phone before an interview began.

But what was this sudden onslaught of new messages? Maybe, at last, he was a finalist for the OGD International Theater Award. The finalists were always announced at the beginning of May. And why not? Structurally, *Even You Are Socrates Now* was his most inventive play, except perhaps for the mounting pile of scenes in his drawer. Maybe he was finally about to have his moment. Lucrative prize news while sipping a latte in Paris, about to speak with a theater critic from *Le Monde*.

But the new messages were not in the language of the country that oversaw the prize. The messages were all in his own language. At the sight of Cristina's name, he felt the shriveling immediately begin within him.

By the time he clicked on the video and saw Victor on the misty dock, he felt nauseous. He watched his brother stagger and wanted to turn away but forced himself to keep watching as Victor dragged some stranger's limp body along the planks. The video was soundless and had the smeary quality of security cameras, but the stiff, determined movements were indisputably Victor's. That was his brother pushing a man off the dock into the water.

You must be Freddy, a voice said with a French accent and Freddy sent his phone clattering to the floor.

The morning was humid and smelled of rain. On the front porch, Lena was gathering up the wine bottles from the night before while Cosmo finished his toast on the front steps. She'd brought him outside to avoid waking Simon on the living room couch, or Sara in the guest room off the kitchen. In the morning, Cosmo was at his most talkative and inquisitive. Today he was intent on hearing why Olga needed a slogan, and why children weren't allowed to vote, and what exactly happened with Oscar's sperm when he came to the island.

We've gone over the sperm question quite a few times now, Lena said as she bagged the last of the wine bottles and grabbed a broom to sweep the popcorn off the porch onto the grass. Do you want to make your own slogan for Olga? I bet she'd love to wake up to a poster from you. Still holding the broom handle, Lena reached for her phone where she'd left it on the banister to see what was happening in the world.

At the top headline, she pressed the broom against her chest. She lowered her finger to the arrow to play the video. Behind her, she heard Cosmo asking something in his high, chirpy voice but it was as if his voice were on a radio in another home and all that was close was the deafening silence of her passive role in the homicide playing out on her phone screen. Some mother's twenty-year-old son. The very age Victor had been when she met him. Nearly the age his Uncle Edgar had been when he'd been caught in the roundups, his body dumped in the very interior she was living in now.

She pressed the arrow of the video again, pressed the broom

handle harder against her chest until it hurt. At the sound of her own child shouting the name Edgar behind her, she felt disoriented until she saw the silver Land Rover slowing at the end of their drive, heard its thick tires crunching over the stones of their unfinished road.

By the time the boys darted into the field, drops of rain had begun to plink audibly against the grass. Both Cristina and Lena stuck to the subject of Olga's campaign until the boys pleaded to run together through the field one more time before Edgar left for the airport. It's the only morning flight, Cristina explained after the children raced off. And I don't want Edgar to overhear what's on the news.

He'll find out eventually, Lena said.

But not yet. Cristina clutched her bag.

They were standing at the edge of the field, under the cover of the trees. The drops were coming faster and harder, falling through the leaves and branches to dampen their arms and faces, Lena still in her pajamas, Cristina with the heavy makeup she'd put on before leaving for the airport. She'd been so relieved to go through the familiar sequence of motions in front of the mirror that she'd kept repeating them and now felt her foundation caking from the humidity.

Please let me know how it goes for Olga, she said. If she doesn't win a spot on the council, I could help her get some other municipal position. My father knows the mayor here. They might even be able to invent some kind of literacy-related position for her—if she'd like that. There's more money coming in now, with all the families moving out from the capital.

Lena thanked her for the offer and Cristina nodded, too exhausted to say any more, and Lena didn't ask her to. They just watched the boys' wheeling arms growing smaller off at the opposite end of the field. Abruptly, their two small bodies slipped out of sight. When a minute passed without any sign of them, Cristina called for them to come back. Then another minute passed, containing within it a whole millennium of sons who'd raced off and never returned.

In the meantime, the rain went on quickening, the leaves providing no cover at all by the time they spotted two little figures bobbing up from a dip in the grass. In silence, they stood and shared the relief of it, the sight of their sons running toward them, returning over the land of the island where they were born.